Golden

BILL DODDS

All characters, names, and incidents
in this book are entirely fictitious.
Well, God is real. But forgiving.
So we think we're on pretty safe ground here.

Copyright © 2020 Bill Dodds

ISBN:
978-0-9840908-6-0
0-9840908-6-X

DEDICATION

To my fellow graduates
of the S.E.S. Class of 1970

Bill A., Kevin C., Paul D. (of happy memory),
Tom E., Mike E., Mitch M., Ed M.,
Paul M., John R., Terry R., and Kurt W.

Thank you, boys.
Boarding school, huh?

1

I had a plan the first time I walked into Brookfield Washington Academy in September 1966. I had a plan all right.

Keep my head down and my mouth shut for three years and then enlist in the Army when I turned eighteen.

Go to Vietnam.

Show them. Whoever they were.

That seemed to be my only thought.

Kill them.

They killed Dad.

So kill them.

Yeah.

A tiny flame deep inside me. Keeping me almost warm. Keeping me barely alive.

Hate has a shiny side.

Here are the basics:

My father, William John Eastman, was a U.S Army master sergeant with twenty-three years in. He made it through the last half of World War II, all of Korea, and one-and-a-half tours in Vietnam.

My mom died when I was three. Natural causes. I have no memories of her except those planted by Grandma. Her mom.

Grandma lived with Dad and me on base when he was stationed in the U.S. And I lived with Grandma at her house when he was deployed overseas. That happened pretty regularly. He wasn't one for sitting still and, God bless him, he wasn't really one for being a father.

But he was *my* father.

You know?

Anyway, Uncle Sam had kept him in Germany through the early '60s but he finally got to go ("got to go"—his words) where the action was.

Killed in action.

Grandma and I got word on June 14. Flag Day. An Army brat knows that kind of stuff.

An officer and a chaplain at the door.

Funeral, cemetery, gun salute, taps. Folded flag. Given to me.

An only child.

Grandma died two months later. Natural causes.

A lonely child.

I suppose I would have gone into foster care for three years but there was a guy, one of Dad's Army buddies, who had agreed to be my legal guardian if ... .

An Army lawyer explained it all to me. Well, told me about it and tried to explain it. The gist of it was I was leaving Des Moines, Iowa, and moving to some little town outside Seattle, Washington.

The buddy, Malcolm Stevenson, worked at a boarding school and I could live there and go to school.

Whatever.

I'd go in as a sophomore but the rest of the class had started as freshmen.

Sure. Of course.

An all-boys school. Grades nine through twelve.

Terrific.

No JROTC. Junior Reserve Officers Training Corps.

Just as well. I didn't want to be an officer. Just a regular grunt… with an M16.

Mr. Stevenson had met me at the airport. He seemed a little older than Dad. Maybe mid-forties. He drove me through Seattle and up around what I'd later learn is Lake Washington. Took me in a back, basement door, which I'd later learn was the workers' entrance.

Not the faculty entrance. The workers' entrance. Blue-collar guys.

He led me up to the first floor to a table that had been set up in the main lobby.

The "foyer."

"This is … " He gave my name to two older students at the table. Then to me: "I have to get back to work. I'll check in with you later." I nodded. He headed off.

The first guy at the table flipped through some papers on a clipboard. Lists. Then he smiled and leaned toward his partner.

"He's sharing a room with the … "

2

I suppose I should have written he said the N-word. Or that he used a racial epithet. But at that time, in that place, he said what he said. Flat out.

The other guy looked up at me and laughed. "Good," he said.

"Scylla and Charybdis," the first guy said and the second guy nodded.

In my junior year—"Third Year" in BWA-speak—I would read some of Homer's works (in translation) and find out Scylla and Charybdis were mythical sea monsters. And referred to a narrow straight that was dangerous to get through.

"So which are you?" the second guy asked.

"Charybdis," I said because I liked the sound of it. That would make Pudge "Scylla."

Turned out he was fine with that. A six-headed monster. More like six-brained. But no monster.

His real first name was Edward. That's what he goes by now. Or did. But he introduced himself to me as Pudge and Pudge he's remained. I consider it a great honor to be among the select few, the inner-inner circle, who call him that. Who get to call him that.

"Okay, Carrie," the first guy said. "Room 427. You can use the elevator if you have a lot of … "

I held up my battered Army-green duffel bag. Barely half full.

Travel light, ready to fight.

"Anyway," the first guy said, "elevator's down the hall and around the corner."

"And welcome to BWA, Carrie," the second guy said.

I found the elevator, pushed the call button, and waited. When the door opened a man in his early thirties in a black-and-gray tweed jacket with black leather patches on the elbows stood staring at me. Black wingtips, cuffed dark gray trousers, button-down-collar white shirt, and light gray bow tie.

Colorful.

I stepped aside so he could exit the car. He just stood there. I just stood there.

"May I help you?" he asked.

Did the elevator operators dress like some kind of stereotypical "professor"?

"Fourth floor, my good man," I said.

"I beg your pardon!"

I assumed he considered me a complete boor, if not also a cad and a bounder.

"This is just for faculty and staff, isn't it?" I asked.

"Faculty. The service elevator is at the far end of the building."

I said nothing.

"Are you making a delivery?" he asked.

I was in tattered, black, low-top Converse sneakers; faded blue jeans; and a not-quite-white T-shirt.

Delivery boy? A good guess. An, *sniff,* educated guess.

"Only myself," I said.

"I beg your pardon?" Clearly not begging. Clearly not even asking.

I knew the welcoming committee duo had been hoping something like this this would happen.

"I'm heading up to my room" I said.

"*Your* room?"

"Four twenty-seven."

"And you are ... ?"

"A new student. Sophomore."

"Second Year."

Okay.

"You are to be a student ... here?" he said. "There is a large public high school in town. Perhaps you have inadvertently, that is to say, by accident, arrived at the wrong institution."

I've been institutionalized!

Wrong place? I wished.

The elevator door started to close and the man shot out his arm to send it back.

I strongly suspected he wanted to do the same to me.

That didn't seem like such a bad idea.

3

I climbed the stairs, headed down the hall, and opened the door to room 427. Slightly larger than a prison cell. I assumed. Institutional-green walls. A small built-in closet. Tiny sink and medicine cabinet. Metal-frame bunk beds. Two narrow wooden dressers. One window. One skinny Black kid looking out it. A dark-black Black kid.

He turned, smiled, and extended his hand.

He told me his name. I told him mine. We took a couple of steps toward each other and shook hands. He had a firm grip. I knew I did, too. (Dad.)

"Although," I said, "the two idjits at the table in the main hall ... "

"'Idjits,'" he said, clearly appreciating the description.

" ... seem to have decided my name is 'Carrie.'"

"Kerry? Like the county in Ireland?"

"I don't know. I was thinking more like the girl's name."

He shrugged. "They called me 'Lips.'" He puckered. "Quite often," he said, "my people are full-lipped."

I didn't know how to respond.

"And," he continued, touching his right cheek, "our skin color is of a darker hue than the mainstream here in the

7

United States."

I leaned in, as if I hadn't noticed, and I saw his eyes brighten.

He touched his hair. I nodded. He touched his nose. "Ah ha," I said.

"Not," he said, "that I would speak ill of those thin-lipped, pasty-faced, straight-haired, needle-nosed ... "

"Idjits."

"Now, now. Mustn't sink to name-calling. But I believe they've been a little hasty in judging me."

I liked him. And, I could tell, he liked me.

I suppose part of what made the difference for me was I had gone to racially-mixed schools on Army bases. The same was true for when I lived with Grandma and went to public schools.

He held out his hand again. "Edward. Family and friends call me 'Pudge.'"

"Jake," I said and we shook hands again.

"You might want to stick with 'Carrie,'" he said. I looked at him. "At some boarding schools 'the jakes' is the term for the restroom."

"Well ... crap."

"On the other hand," he said, "if you stick with your given name you'll fit right in."

John Eastman. That's my name.

"John William Eastman," I said.

"Better still," Pudge said. "Only way to top it would be if your middle name were Windsor."

"So why 'Carrie'?" I said.

He leaned against one of the dressers, crossed his arms, and studied me. "Now, I think we've figured out why they called me 'Lips,'" he said and I couldn't help but laugh. I told him how my exchange with them had gone—leaving out the racial epithet—and Pudge nodded and smiled.

"Got it," he said. "You're Charybdis. Carrie for short."

I sighed and gestured toward the beds. "You want upper

or lower?"

"Doesn't matter."

"You were here first."

He pulled a penny out of his pants pocket. "Heads you take the top, tails I take the bottom."

"I think this game is rigged," I said. "No need to flip."

He opened his eyes wide. They showed a lot of white. "If you say so. We can switch at the end of the semester. At Christmas."

Christmas. I sat down heavily on the lower bunk. Head bowed. Staring at the dark tan linoleum floor. Taking slow, deep, ragged breaths.

A moment passed.

"I was told a little bit about what happened," Pudge said. Softly. "About your dad and gramma."

More ragged breaths.

"I don't know what to say except … " he said and paused. I looked up at him. " … get your butt off my bed."

Just what one fifteen-year-old boy needed to hear from another fifteen-year-old boy.

4

A bell rang. *The* bell. There was one on each of the four floors and in the basement. Thick metal, larger than a dinner plate. More like a medium-sized pizza. It would sound for a minimum of five seconds.

I jumped and Pudge looked startled.

There was a commotion in the hallway as some boys strode purposely toward one of the two stairwells on either end and other guys just looked at each other. It was the difference between Second Year and First Year students.

Second Years cocksure, as sophomores always are. First Years trying to seem brave but looking lost.

First Years and the two of us. Neither fish nor fowl. *Sui generis*. One of a kind. But, fortunately, we were two of a kind. In the same boat. Feeling we were up Poo-Poo Creek without a paddle.

Herd mentality kicked in and we followed those who seemed to know where they were going. The auditorium. Two long aisles. Fold-down seats. Like a movie theater. Seating for some three hundred, quickly becoming two-thirds full.

Two hundred guys. About fifty in each class.

Judging by their ages, it seemed to be Fourth Years in the front center, Third Years on the right side and Second Years on the left. First Years being penned in to the rear center rows, with a couple of empty rows separating them from the Fourth Years.

Sacred space that, apparently, would take First Years three years to cross.

Pudge and I took two seats on the left-side section. Way in the back.

"Carrie," I heard someone say.

"Lips," another said.

We both looked up. The two guys from the "welcoming" table heading for the front-row-center seats.

Pudge stood. "We didn't get your names," he said.

The pair turned. "You can call me Mr. Dickerson and this is Mr. Waddell," one said.

"Got it," Pudge said. Then softly: "Dickwad."

"What did you say!" Mr. Dickerson demanded.

"Dickerson Waddell. Got it."

The older student looked suspicious. And confused. Then decided to look tough in an apparent attempt to cover up both earlier emotions.

"C'mon," Mr. Waddell said. "Who gives a rat's ass about these guys? One more year and we're out of here."

"Already been here for five," I whispered and Pudge bent forward, shoulders shaking in silent laughter.

A kid sitting by himself in the row ahead of us turned around. "'Dickwad.' Nice."

"Just want to do my part for the Class of 1969," Pudge said, sitting up and gasping.

"You can't believe how glad I am to see you guys.

"Yeah?" I asked.

He nodded. "I got here the beginning of First Year second semester. Now I'm not the new kid anymore."

"Happy to oblige," Pudge said.

"We live to serve," I said.

"Dickwad give you a name?" I asked.

"'Eric the Red,'" he said, pointing at his red-headed crewcut.

"Lucky," Pudge said. "Wait. Is your name really Eric?"

"Yeah."

"Lucky," I said.

"Could have been Lucy Ricardo," Eric said.

"Or 'Skelton,'" I said. "I'm John, this is Ed."

He gave a chin-up-once nod. Pudge did the same in return.

Sound-system feedback squealed and most of the two hundred boys put their hands over their ears. "Gentlemen," a man up on the stage said. "Gentlemen!'

"Buckle up," Eric said, imitating Bette Davis. "It's going to be a bumpy night."

5

The fellow at the lectern was tall, slender, and ... academic. A little pale. A little stoop-shouldered. In his fifties. Pleasant. And smiling. Like there was nowhere else on earth he'd rather be.

He talked about the outstanding history and tradition of Brookfield Washington Academy as if it were Oxford and hadn't been founded only thirty years earlier. I had read that in the little brochure Mr. Stevenson had given me.

Maybe Dr. Bradshaw—that was his name—had been on the faculty since the groundbreaking. Worked his way up to ... what? President? Dean? Big Cheese? And succeeded in reaching his life's goal.

Good for him. Good for anyone who does that.

I wondered if Dad had. Died for his country. Was that it?

No. Well, yes. But no. More like died so the guy next to you doesn't die. "Country" can be abstract. The grunt firing right beside you is about as concrete as it can get.

Believe me.

I thought about reaching one's lifetime goal as Dr. Bradshaw talked.

I liked the idea of it. That, somehow, Dad had succeeded.

I still like it.

The Army hadn't given Grandma and me any specifics about his death. Heroic. In service to his fellow soldiers. No pain, gone in an instant. Sounded a bit boilerplate but a comforting boilerplate.

"He fought for me," Pudge whispered.

Dad? No ... him? Dr. Bradshaw?

I pictured the good professor in battle fatigues. Lobbing a grenade. Crawling through a tunnel. Apparently Pudge noticed my confusion.

"Integrating the hallowed halls of BWA," Pudge said.

I looked around at the other students.

"I'm a raisin in this bowl of rice," Pudge said.

"God have mercy on your soul," Eric said without turning around. "Hard enough just being a redhead."

Pudge reached forward and rubbed Eric's head. "For good luck," he said.

"Just don't give me any crap about leprechauns or Lucky Charms, okay?"

"Long as you don't call me 'Buckwheat.'"

"Deal." Then: "So what about G.I. Joe here?"

"Too close to home," Pudge said and he leaned forward and spoke quietly to Eric.

"Oh, double crap," Eric said. "Sorry, John."

"It's okay. Just share some of your marshmallow bits."

"Kiss off."

Even then I knew I had lucked out with these two guys. A pretty profound thought for a teenage boy.

It's one that's never left me.

At the fiftieth class reunion—and that's coming up fast now—these were the only guys I wanted to see. Just them And Dr. Bradshaw. But, God rest his soul. He didn't make it to one hundred plus.

I'm still on the fence about going. Looks like Eric is a yes. But Pudge hasn't committed yet. The BWA fat-cat alumni and board of trustees have opened it up to become an all-school reunion, trying to entice him. And take advantage of him.

Which, I'm sure, he finds as amusing as I do.

Probably more so.

In recent years the raisin became "one of ours"!

Then, too, maybe his little sister will be there. Be very good to see her. See if that still rankles an older—and protective—brother.

But I'm getting ahead of myself here.

6

The only people who *like* meetings are the people who *run* the meetings.

But... not all people who *run* meetings *like* meetings.

Therefore we can conclude ... .

I'm sure there's some logic point ("logic," is that the right word?) to be made with those two statements but my point here is that right after we had that first-day gathering in the auditorium ...

Wait.

This is another example of why BWA (Brookfield Washington Academy) could be such a ...

Wait. Again.

Now that I think of it, BWA could have stood for Bigoted White A**holes. (I can't include the S and S in the last word because of Grandma. As the twig is bent ... .)

And Pudge never would have gone along with that. Not with the mom he had.

There's a reason I'm rambling like an old man here. I *am* an old man here. "Only" in my sixties but it's only people who are in their sixties who consider it "only." Well, maybe people in their seventies and eighties do.

But for fifteen-year-olds—which is what Pudge, Eric, and I were on that September morning—sixty might as well have been a thousand. Most, if not all, of the faculty members were in their twenties through fifties and they were old.

Some were ancient.

And now Pudge, Eric, and I are older than each of them was then.

I did get a very good education that year. But little of it was in BWA classrooms.

What was I talking about?

Right.

Meetings.

No, first a little more BWA-speak. I soon learned the faculty and student body hadn't gathered in the school auditorium. We met in the theater. But wait! Not just any old theater (like the Bijou or Ingersoll), we were in the Walter Milton Cox Theatre. T-H-E-A-T-R-E.

How that populace loved all things British in this, our own little Eton on the shores of Lake Washington.

The room wasn't named after actor/comedian Wally Cox. (Wallace Maynard Cox.)

But in tribute to Walter Milton "Moneybags" Cox. Class of '46.

Holy Moses, that was only twenty years before I showed up there. So he was probably thirty-nine at the time. In theory, it's possible he could be at the all-school reunion. In his nineties, which is old in anyone's book.

But back to this book. Or whatever it is or will be.

The students filed out of the "theatre" in the shuffling, shoving, "sh*t"-filled language way that's second nature to any all-boys high school, and were herded into separate locations based on year.

Eric, the good shepherd, helped Pudge and me.

Correction. Fourth Years stayed in the theatre. They had earned it! Huzzah for them! Class of 1967, huzzah!

There was an order of privilege, of course. Third Years went to the "best" classroom and First Years were led to the "worst." We poor-sap Second Years went to some sort of Goldilocks place: not the best, not the worst, but just right for us.

So this was "us."

Some fifty guys who walked loud and proud as if they owned the world because they were no longer First Years. In so many places and in so many ways, is there anyone cockier than a sophomore?

I realize now how grateful I am that actor/screenwriter Sylvester Stallone was only twenty at the time and his first films were a ways off. Otherwise, sure as sure can be, when Pudge and I entered that room we would have been greeted with some variation of "It's Sambo and Rambo."

I take that back.

I'm not sure anyone in the class was that clever.

Except for Eric, Pudge, and me.

7

One of the advantages of being an Army brat is you've gone to Department of Defense Dependents Schools all over the country if not the world. (D.o.D.D.S., which is about the stupidest acronym ever.)

Yes, once in a great while you make friends quickly but even then you know you or they will be moving on soon. But ... you do get pretty good at sizing up people. And in every class—say a bunch of Second Year guys—you know there are going to be a few decent people, a lot who are okay, and some who are absolute jerks.

Or worse.

You develop a sense of D.o.D.D.S. radar and can quickly spot the blips: the jerks. In the fall of 1966 at Brookfield Washington Academy, Aston Aston lit up the screen.

Yes, that was his name. His grandfather had been a U.S. senator and Secretary of Commerce, and his father was the current governor.

Aston Aston, Sr.

Aston Aston, Jr.

And Aston Aston III.

The last now Second Year class president.

Hail to the Chief.

Past experience in the world of academia had taught me to keep my big trap shut when Aston Aston III began our little get-together by reviewing his pedigree.

The son of a b ...

I assumed the lesson in lineage was for Pudge's and my benefit.

Pudge nodded and looked impressed.

I smiled. That is, I moved my lips so the ends lifted a tad. Much to my credit, what I did not do was say:

"Wow, that's a ton of ass."

My radar said A3 was more than a little displeased that *his* class now had a Negro and a white-trash waif. Yes, he'd make the best of it—stiff upper lip—but he pointed out:

"And to those who are new to the academy I feel it only right and proper to warn you our academic standards are rigorous."

("Our.")

Some four dozen boys turned to look back where Pudge, Eric, and I were seated. Apparently Eric, despite already completing one semester there, was still suspect.

"'Rigris'?" I said in a loud voice, shifting to my "confused face" and lifting my hand to be recognized and ask my question.

Eric, sitting next to me, whispered, "Here we go," because he knew what was funny and my response was funny. I didn't look at Pudge but I had no doubt his eyes sparkled.

A3 shook his head and chuckled softly because he thought my obvious stupidity was sad but amusing and not unexpected. And so, of course, about three-quarters of the class started laughing.

Which, it is interesting to note (to use an academic phrase), in circumstances such as these that sound can easily be mistaken for the noise of sycophants kissing a higher-up's rear end. In this case it wasn't mistaken. That's exactly what it was.

"*Rig*-or-us," A3 said, playing to the crowd. His crowd.

My face remained the same. My hand shot up a second time.

"Yes?" he said. Benevolent.

"I'm supposed to choose one or the other?"

"What?" he asked.

"Those aca-demonic things are supposed to be 'rig' or they're supposed to be 'us' and I'm supposed to choose which?"

"No," he said. *Eek!* Flustered. A little confused.

Heads swirled. Eyes fixed forward. And some guys laughed. Really laughed.

The new kid, the white one, had skewered Aston Aston III.

I should have kept my mouth shut.

8

It's funny how thinking about old times, and writing down an incident or two, stir up more memories. Some good. Some so very bad.

I can tell you that in 1966 there was zero grief counseling for a fifteen-year-old boy. At least for this fifteen-year-old.

A half dozen year later there was little or nothing for ... .

But that was part three of my life. This is about part two.

This writing of a half-baked memoir is, I suppose, my figuring out if I'm going back to part two for my fiftieth reunion. I waver.

Yeah, sure why not?

No. Never. Only fifty? Not in a million.

Okay, some basics. Students were required to wear dark gray slacks, white dress shirt, dark-red and light-gray striped (school colors) tie, and a navy-blue blazer with the BWA crest on the breast pocket. It was the uniform of the day (though never called that) for all official times and occasions. Including classes.

With black socks and black, lace-up shoes. Leather, of course.

My shoes were the best polished. Some guys noticed and they paid me to shine theirs. I suppose some thought it was amusing to have the charity case shining shoes. And others thought it should have been Pudge doing the job. Either way, I charged them for it and took pleasure in spitting on their shoes (for a better shine, of course) and sometimes in their shoes (just for my own sake).

To me it was a princely sum but to the young princes at BWA it was chump change.

I, of course, being that chump.

I tried to split the take with Pudge but he turned me down. We had been standing together on the quad when a junior, excuse me, a Third Year, approached me. Asked if I could do his shoes and what it would cost. I told him and Pudge said, "A little more for the deluxe."

The upperclassman was used to living a deluxe lifestyle.

I doubled my fee.

"For the front," Pudge told the guy. "Twice that for the whole shoe."

The boy nodded.

"Per shoe," Pudge said.

Another nod.

I ended up doing about ten pairs a week. Sometimes more than one pair for the same guy. (Who would have only one pair of black shoes? Why, the very thought of it!)

I tried to get Pudge to let me polish his. He just smiled and shook his head.

"Why not?"

"Ask me that after you meet my parents." Then he looked like he had stepped in something.

Parents. I had none. Family. I had none.

I asked: "Your folks know you need the practice because it's going to be your full-time job once you're out of here?"

He smiled. Relieved.

"Tell them not to get their hopes up," I said.

I'm pretty sure Pudge has somebody who polishes his shoes now but I wouldn't bet on it. Even at age fifteen he was pretty set in his ways.

They were good ways.

I'm sure they still are.

I'd bet on that.

Dear Lord, I'm rambling on and on like an old far … .

9

It would help if I could leaf through a few of the school's year books from way back when. I tossed mine not long after graduation. I didn't take much with me.

Nothing to slow me down.

Classes. Maybe something here about what classes Second Year guys took. That, I remember.

Latin, English, biology, geometry, and economics.

Economics?

Yes. For four years. Or three in my case. The school's founders and current board of trustees knew which side their bread was buttered on. (If I were more clever I'd make some comment here about their (fat) butts being breaded.)

I would estimate that at least eighty percent of the boys came from families that took economics very seriously.

(It was their bread and butter. Enough of that!)

They were old money, fairly recent money (a few generations), and nouveau riche. And they wanted their young princes to step forward (in shiny shoes) as titans of industry and commerce. I realize now, but it certainly didn't occur to me then, there was a lot of pressure on those guys.

The typical story was someone, long ago or recently, made

a ton of money (legally or through, *ahem*, less that lawful means) and the family had guarded it and made it grow. Now it was up to assorted knuckleheads in BWA blazers to do the same. Not just keep it. But make it bigger.

I suppose that's the way it is in a lot of families.

A tradition of service to others.

Of academia.

Of healthcare.

Of military service.

Whoa, that one hits home.

From time to time over the years, I've wondered what my life would have been like if Dad hadn't been in the Army. Or if he hadn't died fighting for the guy next to him.

If Mom hadn't died when I was so little. If Grandma hadn't died when I was… taller than she was but still little.

If I hadn't been made a ward of one of Dad's buddies. Hadn't attended BWA. Hadn't met Pudge and his family. Or Eric and his.

How different a person would I be now?

I'm going to blame it on the meds. This mental wandering here. I was writing about classes and I find myself thinking of some parallel, possible life that never happened.

So, anyway, economics was a big deal there. Running a business, a commercial empire, not just how to balance a checkbook or plan a family's weekly budget.

Yes, there must have been pressure on the little titans-in-training. I know they "had" to get into the right universities and they were already in a hole when it came to that.

The "hole" being BWA.

Yes, it was hot stuff in Washington state but … Washington state?

Yes, Boeing, PACCAR and some others but … . They were big but most other local industries were small potatoes compared to other parts of the country. The North*east* comes to mind.

BWA was a feeder school to the Ivy League but BWA was figuratively and literally in the sticks. (One hundred eighty acres of forest bordering Lake Washington. (On which body of water, to the south, Bill Gates would later set up his homestead. Young Bill was not a BWA student.)

I'm sure a lot of my classmates would have considered themselves failures, and their fathers would have agreed, if they didn't get accepted at one of the "right" schools.

Just as, likewise, I would have considered myself a failure if I hadn't … .

We were all so young.

What did we know?

Pudge and I did know this:

Most of the students and a large chunk of the faculty wanted the two of us out. As soon as possible.

10

Pudge wasn't going to let that happen because of his own family responsibilities.

I wasn't because all I wanted to do was fight. Here or Nam. Here for three years. There for two tours. Two *full* tours. At least.

Hooah!

What about Eric? He was welcomed by the board and faculty because his family was L-O-A-D-E-D. North. South. East. West. National. Global. Not that you'd know it from talking to him. Not that, sad to say, he was accepted by a lot of his peers. I suspect they were jealous because his family was far wealthier than theirs.

I wouldn't have used the word at the time, but looking back I can see he was really sweet. A deep-seated kindness that could absorb or deflect a lot of teasing and just keep smiling. It didn't have to do with the money. It was just him.

It wasn't that he was rich. Which he was.

It was that he was so deeply loved by his family. Which he was.

It was illness that had kept him out of BWA for the first semester of high school. Instead, he was home schooled. A phrase not used much back then and one that, it seems to me, would have been inaccurate in his case. He was mansion schooled.

Now he was herded into a classroom just like the rest of us. After I got to know him better I asked if he missed being tutored at home instead of stuck at BWA.

"No, this is okay," he said. "And tutoring was okay, too." He shrugged. "You know."

But I didn't.

All right, now I'm really going to focus. I'm really going to try to focus. On Second Year classes.

Latin. Julius Caesar.

I had taken freshman Latin at a public school. Grandma's idea. I thought it had been a little stupid. But now I realized it kept me from having to be in First Year Latin with the little ones. Thank you, Grandma.

Instead I was spending time learning that Gaul, as a whole, was divided into three parts.

"BWA," a voice in the back of the classroom said in a stage whisper," *is a hole* divided into four years."

The prof just smiled. He'd been down this road more than a few times. At least a dozen. Mr. Clayborn.

"I assume that's 'hole' without a W," he said and the class laughed. Gumby was all right. (Clayborn to Clay-man to Gumby. Tall and slender.)

Every faculty member had a nickname. Some not—to use an expression that came later—"rated G."

"Yes, sir," the whisperer said.

"Good to see you're applying a classical reference to a modern situation," he said.

"Yes, sir."

"And are you ready to do a little translating of *The Gallic Wars* for us?"

"Yes, sir."

"Good."

Not a punishment, just moving on with the lesson.

I sat there thinking I would be better off learning Vietnamese.

11

I'll get to writing about the other classes but, just like a kid in school, first I want recess. Or, at BWA, competitive sports. I want to talk about them.

There was no physical education but intramural (among ourselves) and intermural (with other schools) sports. Coming from the Latin *intra* and *inter*. (Thank you, Gumby.)

I don't remember where *mural* fits in. No matter. I didn't make any intermural teams my first year … as a Second Year. I did truly enjoy a rousing game of smash-mouth with my classmates.

No. *Against* my classmates. Again, not all. But some.

And they, it was immediately clear, enjoyed the same against Pudge and me.

Eric, still not completely recovered, sat out the first season.

Football.

God, that was fun.

Hold on. I need to explain something else. There were those at BWA, both faculty and students, who referred to football as "American football."

Blimey!

"Real football" was soccer because that was what civilized white males played in England. Never mind the rest of the world with all those gents of many, many hues and colors.

Soon after the end of World War II, BWA tried to form a soccer team but, how to put this, the students were horrible at it, didn't like it, and there were no other schools with which to compete.

Ditto with lacrosse.

And cricket.

So the seasons were football, basketball, baseball, and—on one day—track and field.

I have no idea why I'm writing this. What can it possibly matter? Either I'll go to the reunion or I won't. I doubt Pudge will be there. And I still see Eric and his wife every once in a while.

Wow. Ten years ago. No. Hmm. A year ago?

This getting old stuff is getting old.

Let me see if I can come up with a typical example (I would say "archetypical" if I were writing about an English class) of intramural football in the fall of 1966.

And let's call it "Death on the Fifty Yard Line: Game One."

I can't believe the strength and stamina I had at that time. I, who just returned here to the computer keys after a ninety-minute nap. Ninety minutes! I run out of steam and my mind goes with it.

Maybe I should have told you (whoever you are) how teams were chosen. It wasn't strictly by year in school but by talent. (Some half-baked "tryouts.")

Or friends.

Same as with so much of life.

Tigers, Bears, Eagles … and … two more. Three more? Pudge and I were Eagles. Third string, which meant mostly classmates but some a year older and a few a year younger.

This shouldn't be so hard to explain. Say there were five teams with four strings and each string had two squads.

I think I have this right, after pulling out a piece of scratch paper and a pen: 200 (students) divided into 5 (teams) equals 40 (team members) divided by 4 (strings) equals 10 (guys) to a squad. But that can't be right. The twenty best in the whole school were on the school team not on some squad.

Squad.
BWA wasn't the last time I was assigned to a squad.

12

I'm sure those kinds of details aren't important but, it seems, sometimes as I write this I get distracted. Or something.

Team T-shirts but no helmets, pads, or other protective gear except a jock strap under a pair of jeans or sweatpants.

Quarterback. Center. Couple linemen. Couple wide receivers.

Touch not tackle. Or, more accurately, "slamming" not tackle. "Touching" the guy who carried the ball was a lot like a tackle in tackle football. And a "touch" could be administered with a hand, a fist, an elbow, and so on.

Immediately followed by a shove, a knee, a cleated shoe.

Refs were Fourth Year guys. Not exactly impartial but near mayhem is better than complete mayhem.

I loved it. Most guys played offense *and* defense and that was just fine by me. More opportunities to lay out someone right on his butt.

I've already mentioned grief in the mid-1960s and how it was handled. For me, that fall it was more manhandling. There was this sweet feeling of crushing someone. And of purposely letting some defensive lineman flash right by me and cause quarterback Aston Aston III great consternation.

He didn't want Pudge and me on his squad, his string, his team. But there we were. Later—I don't know if someone told me or I just figured it out—it was clear some of the Fourth Years thought he was … well, exactly what he was … and this was their way to stick it to him.

I was happy to make them happy but it would have been so great to have been lining up against him as he received the ball from the center.

So great.

No one told me that grieving can include a lot of anger. A brutal emotion that has to go somewhere. Out or in. Or both. Mine was both but I didn't know it. I didn't know what was going on at least half the time of that first year at BWA.

At least.

No mom. No dad. No grandma. Nothing familiar. Nothing comforting. Not knowing what I was going through and having no one around me even acknowledging the giant fecal storm that had become my life.

(The use of "fecal" here as a small gesture of love and respect for Grandma.)

No. Now that I write this I know that's not completely true. Yes, no one around me knew what I was going through but there was Pudge and Eric. ("There were"?) I don't think I would have survived, and I mean that, survived without them. And without their families.

From fall 1966 to spring 2019 I have been, and remain, in their debt. My life has not been perfect. Parts have been far from carefree.

But I think it would have ended that fall so long ago. I think I would have ended it.

Had it not been for them.

13

Well, that got pretty maudlin. Been a while since the tears didn't just well up in my eyes but ran down my cheeks, too. Who knew poking at an old wound, scraping at an old scar, could make an old pain so fresh again?

Let's talk about something else. What about Pudge on the football field? 'Twas grand, as Grandma used to say. 'Twas truly grand.

I never saw him break a rule but he could dance along its edge just as he did carrying the ball down the sideline without ever stepping out of bounds.

Fleet of foot and sly as a fox. With big, brown, "innocent" eyes. So young to have learned the fine and delicate art of faking sincerity.

I'm not putting it right. That sounds as if Pudge was two-faced and he never was. He was absolutely honest but people heard what they wanted to hear.

I'll give you an example. This was, oh, maybe sometime in late November. Yes. Before the Thanksgiving break.

The two of us were summoned to the headmaster's office and on the way I wondered out loud if we were going to be sacked.

"I don't think so," he said.

"What makes you so sure?"

"I'm an excellent student and a true asset to the school."

"Uh huh. And me?"

"You? Well, it's clear I've been willing to carry you."

"So kind." I said.

"I know. 'He ain't heavy but he's no brutha.'"

"Uh huh."

"Now," he said, "just follow my lead."

We knocked on the headmaster's office door, were given permission to enter, and waved into two armless hard wooden chairs. Facing His Highness.

"I suppose you're wondering why I summoned you," he said.

I had learned quite a bit about living in a boarding school over the past eight weeks or so. Dr. Bradshaw, the fellow who ran the joint and had been the main act at our introductory assembly was the "headmaster."

And, my first instincts about him seemed to be right. He was okay. All things considered.

Now, apparently, he wanted to chat a little about "all things." Check up, check in, on how the rich white wave was treating us … uh … non-rich or non-white folks.

"I'll be blunt, boys," he said. "Has there been any unexpected nastiness aimed at you since your arrival?"

Ball's in your court, Pudge, I thought.

He was silent. I was silent. He held a steady gaze on Dr. Bradshaw. I held a steady gaze on Dr. Bradshaw. Well, with a few quick side glances at my roommate.

Nastiness. Nice. Not prejudice, hate, or physical abuse.

Nastiness.

Many, many years later I would read the biography of a girl who had integrated a white public high school in the South in the late 1950s.

Nastiness.

Most, though not all, overt.

Not so at BWA. Here, so far, it had been mostly—though not completely—covert. Subtle, refined, genteel prejudice, hate, or physical abuse. (Note to self: More on all that later.)

"No, sir," Pudge said.

To my great credit I didn't gasp or blurt out a sentence that would have begun with "What the ... " and ended with a short word starting with the sixth letter of the alphabet. That is: F.

"No, sir," I said.

"Good, good," Dr. Bradshaw said, relief showing on his face. "So I, I guess that's all for now."

We were dismissed.

14

Back in the hallway, alone and out of the headmaster's earshot, I leaned in to Pudge and sharply whispered, "What the ... forest fire!"

"Nice," he said. "A double F."

It was a game he, Eric, and I had invented and enjoyed playing. The three of us. The F-word was extremely popular at BWA but between Pudge's mother, my grandmother, and Eric's ... whole family ... we were determined to avoid using it.

In some ways, I assume now, to set ourselves apart and above the rich, white riffraff. (Eric was two out of three. He had class.)

"You lied!" I said to Pudge.

"What?"

"You lied to him."

"When?" he asked.

"When? Just now," I said.

"I did no such thing."

"You ... you ... you ..."

"I answered his question honestly," Pudge said.

I was silent. Waiting. Pretty interested in how it wasn't a

lie.

"Think, Jake," he said. A name only he and Eric sometimes used when no one else was around. (The BWA cans *were* called "jakes.")

He patiently continued. "Has any nastiness been aimed at you since your arrival?"

"Sometimes seems like nothing but," I said.

"Me, too."

"So you lied," I said.

"Of course not. Lying is wrong. It's a sin."

Again I waited.

"Did any of it surprise you?" No. I shook my head.

"Are you sure?" he asked.

"I figured it would come," I said, "and, oh yeah, it came."

"Exactly. So how would *you* have honestly answered Dr. Bradshaw: 'Has there been any *unexpected* nastiness aimed at you since your arrival?'?"

Pudge would have made one crackerjack lawyer.

Apparently, I'm not going to write this in strict chronological order. I'm skipping around because my brain, my memories, are skipping around

Plus, at this point, focusing and I are not as one.

What else? Maybe another class. English. I always liked English. At one point—well, more than one point—I thought I'd be a writer.

Come back from serving in Vietnam and write a novel that would … what? I don't know. But it'd be great.

Turned out part of my "issues" after I was discharged was not being able to stop thinking about, obsessing on, my time there. What happened there. The same held true for so many others.

Tough, no, impossible to write about something when you're over-focused on it. When doing that quickly sends you over the edge. (Another note to self: More about that later. Maybe. Maybe not.)

15

Second Year English. Portia Gunderson, Ph.D. That is, Mrs. Ronald Gunderson.

It occurs to me now—Lordy, I'm a slow learner—that *Dr.* Gunderson was always addressed as *Mrs.* Gunderson. I highly doubt by choice. BWA did make one slight day-to-day concession—"Mrs. *Portia* Gunderson"—on the nameplate outside her classroom door. No "Ronald."

And, it goes without saying, it was "Portia Gunderson, Ph.D." in the school catalog, and whenever and wherever else it was, *haff kaff*, financially advantageous.

B! W! A! Go, A**holes!

And how to depict that mascot? Yikes! Perhaps a small donkey with its tail cut very short.

Dr. or Mrs., she learned us gooder than most of the profs there. (My, I'm being silly today. Maybe I'm in a good mood. New meds kicked in?) Seriously, I'd go to the reunion if it were being held right now. (The feeling will pass.)

Description. Today we will write a description. *Description is a form of writing whose purpose is to create pictures, sounds, smells, and touch sensations in the reader's imagination.*

Amazing what a mind can't forget … and repeatedly fails to remember.

Dr. Gunderson was "old." Probably forty. Average height and weight, slightly graying hair. Wife and mother of two girls. A kind face. A person able to absorb and deflect a lot of crap thrown at her.

A good person. A self-confident person, and rightly so.

Okay, here's more about the classroom setup. (I am all *over* the place.) Desks in rows, students in alphabetical order left to right from the prof's point of view. So some poor, suffering souls have to sit in front of, behind, or next to Pudge. Ditto with my desk. Unless either of us was next to the wall or the beginning or end of row.

Anyway … I mention that here because class president A3 (come to think of it he could have embodied the BWA mascot) was always in a front seat. And on this particular day very early in the school year, very early in the class period, he demanded in a loud voice: "Mrs. *Goon*-derson?"

Not raising his hand. Interrupting. Now turning in his seat, playing to the crowd. His people. They now not quite *quietly* whispering their approval.

Now here's an example of why I could never have been a teacher. I would have answered: "Raise your hand and wait until you're called on, Mr. Assss-ton."

"Yes, Mr. Aston?" she said.

"Why do we have to have Julius Caesar in Latin class *and* in this class?"

"That's an interesting question," Dr. Gunderson said to him and then looked around the room and nodded a couple of times. Like, don't we all agree that's very interesting?

I was pretty sure we didn't.

"Why do you think?" she asked him. *Ball's in your court, chump.* That being my thought. I'm sure, not hers.

He shrugged. "I dunno. Seems sort of stupid."

A few chuckles from the audience.

"You don't know?" Dr. Gunderson asked, sounding concerned. "Do you really think they're the same?" (Like, is something wrong with you? Do we need to get you tested?)

"Well … ."

"Just one thing, Mr. Aston. I know you can do this. Just name one way the presentations of Julius Caesar are different in Mr. Bowen's class and in my class."

(Well, shoot, I should have mentioned in her class we were going to be reading Shakespeare's play about old Caesar.)

"Uh … ." A3 now seeming a bit flustered. Somehow challenged in a very unchallenging way. "One is in Latin and one is in English."

Greeted with howls, the howlers assuming he meant one in Latin class and one in English class.

Again turning in his seat. "I mean in the languages." Clarifying, defending himself, and—I'm pretty sure—trying to find out who was laughing at him.

"Good," Dr. Gunderson said. "Absolutely correct. Yes, start with the basics. We have two languages here. That's a foundational difference."

He sat up a little straighter.

"What else?" she asked, looking at me.

Now this was a dilemma.

16

"Ma'am?" I said.

"What's a difference?" As if she knew I knew. Which I did. But how did she know that? I was trying to be so careful.

Head down. Never volunteer.

"Come on, John," she said, not "Mr. Eastman." I wondered if anyone noticed … besides Pudge and Eric.

Jumping into the deep end.

"One describes a series of martial campaigns, the other an assassination. Both with the same protagonist, written more than a millennium and a half apart."

Well … crap.

"That's good, too," she said, as if Aston and I made equal contributions to the day's discussion. See? A good person.

"Oh, horse shhhhhhoes," Aston said, which I thought was an absolutely brilliant save on his part.

"Mr. Aston?" she said. "And, by the way, a lovely epithet."

No doubt that term sailed right over most of the students' heads.

"Yeah," he said. "There's an introduction to the Latin one and it doesn't say anything about a marshal or his running for re-election of something like that."

Eric tried to turn a one-note laugh—"Ha!"—into a sneeze. He failed.

"Good, Mr. Aston," Dr. Gunderson said. "Very clever. Let's talk about homonyms."

"Home-oh *what!*" one kid said, making more than a few classmates laugh.

Not A3.

"And now to Greek!" Dr. Gunderson said. Pleased once again.

Thrust, parry and … well, if I knew more fencing terms I'd use them here.

"In Latin 'homo' means man. You know that. In Greek 'homos' means … ?"

The class was silent. I don't know how she did that. But they were. I was.

Eric raised his hand.

"Mr. Matthews?"

"It means the same."

"The same as the Latin?" she teased?

"No," he said, liking her joke.

"No," she agreed and wrote on the board: the same. She underlined it. "That's the definition for the Greek word."

More writing. "So homonym … " underlining the first syllable once and the second twice " … means the same name. The second from the Greek." She wrote something on the board. In Greek letters. And then "onoma" underneath it.

"Onama, name," she said. "Homonyms. Words that sound alike but are spelled differently and have different meanings. "Marshal, referring to an officer of the law. And … what?"

She looked at me.

Crap again.

"Martial," I said and spelled it out. "Like Mars, the Roman god of *war*."

I thought maybe I had put a little too much oomph in the

last word."

She gave me a sad look. Concerned. Kind.

17

I was sure a lot of the faculty and students—perhaps all of the faculty, students, *and* workers—knew I was an orphan whose father had died in Vietnam.

What I didn't want anyone to know was my plan to reach age eighteen, join the Army, and head for that very place.

It bothered me that Dr. Gunderson seemed to know that. But I couldn't figure out how she knew.

And!

I was doing a very lousy job of keeping my head down and not volunteering. For a guy who isn't dumb I'm not very smart. Twice already I had let my animosity toward Aston Aston III lead me to … . Honestly? To show off. *Look at me! I can slice and dice someone with my witty words and I know a lot of junk.*

Things got worse.

The bell rang for the end of class, we all shuffled out into the main hall, and Mike Behr slid in behind me, lifted my right arm straight up in the air and shouted, "There's a new sheriff in town, boys. I mean marshal."

Ah, for the love of … . Just leave me alone.

Still, it was nice when some guys cheered. Guys, I was

sure, who weren't great A3 fans. His followers were silent. A3 marshalled his dignity—*ha!* see what I did there?—and chose to storm(troop) off.

Nowhere to run to. Nowhere to hide.

Not him. Me.

Then everyone down one flight of stairs to the basement, to the biology/chemistry lab. On the bright side, A3 and I weren't lab partners. On the dark side, his second-in-command (his shadow)—Greg Taylor—and I were.

"Hey," I said to him when we were on stools, side-by-side, "I didn't mean to … "

"Fork you." Well. Not "fork."

I looked across the room at A3. He glanced my way and made a big production of rubbing his nose with only his middle finger.

So … apparently his guys had received their marching orders. And my guys—I did not want "guys"!—were spiritedly using "da daaa, daaa da da da" to sing the theme music to *Gunsmoke*.

Pudge came over and said, "Hey, Taylor, I know you're not someone who … "

"Get out of my face, jigaboo."

Not the first time he had been called that at BWA, but this time was different.

"Uh huh," Pudge said. "Just one more thing. If you like, you and I can get together behind the pop shack after last class this morning and, you know, settle our differences. Just the two of us."

The white boy turned whiter.

"Hey, I … I … I mean … I … "

"Eastman and I are friends," Pudge said. "Got it?"

Greg Taylor nodded.

"A team," Pudge said. "Otherwise … fork you."

With "fork."

The bell rang.

From the front of the room: "Gentlemen. Now open your

books to page ... "
More than a few groans.

18

I suppose I could tell you about biology class but I really don't care for science. In theory, it's fascinating. In reality, for me, it's just a bunch of nitpicky facts.

Pudge didn't bother going over behind the pop shack—I just accidentally typed "pope shack." *Ha!*, again.

Since, I assume no one is ever going to read this I don't feel completely obligated to explain every (nitpicky) detail or reference. On the other hand, if I'm writing this to somehow help me maybe I should.

On the third hand? I'm not sure why I'm doing this.

The pop shack was a small, ancient, standalone building behind the gym that had pop, candy, and ice cream vending machines.

Sorry, Dr. Gunderson.

That had vending machines filled with pop, candy, and ice cream.

After the last class that morning, Pudge, Eric, and I were out on the front steps talking about everything and nothing when Eric asked, "You're not going to go see if Taylor is back there?"

"No. He won't be."

"You sure?" I asked.

"No doubt."

"How come?"

"He's racist," Pudge said.

"So why wouldn't he get a bunch of his buddies to go with him and all pound you?" Eric asked. A good question.

"Because Jake and I are friends, roommates, and fellow outcasts."

"So?" Eric said.

"So you would be there and—no offense, but more importantly—Jake would be there."

"So?"

"So Jake's posse would be there, too. Right, Marshal?"

The two of them laughed till tears rolled down their faces. When they finally stopped Eric managed, "Deputize us, Jake" and they were off again.

Writing this makes no sense. Maybe I should be doing it by themes or something, not some helter-skelter memories.

Themes. Like … racism. And … illness. Not that I know anything about them but my two best friends … .

Huh.

My two best friends in tenth grade.

My two best friends in high school.

My two best friends in my whole life.

Yes, I had others. In boot camp. In Vietnam. At the post office. (Sort of.)

None of them quite like Eric and Pudge. In the Army, two fellow grunts were a very close second, but not like Eric and Pudge.

I would like to see those two classmates again.

I hope I'm able to see them again.

Okay, I should write some more today. More of my story.

My life. My …

Boy, I use a lot of ellipses. Dot, dot, dot. Sorry, Mrs. Gunderson. Doctor. But looking back you seem more like a Mrs., more like a mom.

A mom.

I could write about that. Not that I know, from personal experience. My earliest memories are from kindergarten and I have only a couple of them. Taking a nap on a little rug on the floor. And a playground with teeter-totters.

I'm pretty sure I mentioned Mom died when I was three. So (insert ellipsis here) no memories of her. I do have a memory of her picture. One of Mom and Dad and me. Taken, I presume, by Grandma.

I suppose I still have that around here somewhere. I'm going to go look for it.

Yeah.

"Dear St. Anthony, please look around," Grandma used to say/pray, "something is lost and cannot be found."

I am lost and …

(Another one, dot, dot, dot, Mrs. G.)

I need to stop.

19

Thank you, Tony!

I spent a good chunk of yesterday afternoon digging though boxes and snuffling through drawers and I *found* it.

A square, three inches per side with a white scalloped boarder. Now in a frame next to my laptop. In a 4 x 6 inch frame. You're probably not going to find a 3 x 3 at a local store.

("And do you have any typewriter ribbon?")

Shoot! I bet I could have found it online and had it here in two days. Oh, well. I wasn't raised in a digital world. For my tombstone: *John W. (Jake) Eastman. He was analog.*

On the back of the photo: "1954." Grandma's handwriting. I'd guess on or around my third birthday.

Mom wouldn't see my fourth.

Dad wouldn't see my fifteenth.

Grandma wouldn't see my sixteenth.

Talk about "themes." How about grief? I have some experience there. You betcha.

Anyway, it's nice to have the photo out. On display. Dear Lord, they were young. Mom twenty-three and Dad twenty-nine.

But they look old. No. They look mature. They look like grown-ups.

I found another picture yesterday. A "snapshot." There's an old-timey word.

Vietnam. Me between a Black guy and a white guy. (Kind of a pattern here, huh?) In the boonies. Dressed for it. Dork, Jam, and Buddha.

Privates First Class Donald Baxter, John Eastman, and Gregory McIntyre. In-country. They look weary and worn but young.

Old men's eyes looking out from young men's faces.

Two of those names chiseled into the face of a black wall in Washington, D.C.

I went there. One time. To see them. I mean the names. That tore me up. That sent me spiraling down, down, down, and down.

That almost did me in. I almost did myself in.

More than twenty years ago. On that day, more than twenty years since we had been in … there.

When I got back to the States I never contacted anyone in their families. I never tried. I wish I had. At least tried. At least.

Hey, Analog Boy! Pull your head out of your arse and do an Internet search.

I could do that. I mean, their folks are probably dead but maybe a brother or sister. None of us was married. No kids. But they had family. I didn't but they did.

Hey, Tony! One more little favor. Two.

Not for me. Well, for me but for them. Well, not them but whoever was left behind.

It is so hard to be left behind. So incredibly hard.

I'm going to keep typing here and maybe I'll remember one of their brother's or sister's names. Someplace to start.

Where they were from. Dork, Philly. Buddha? Drawl. Barbecue. Texas. Near Austin.

Ha! Of course. Buda, Texas. Pronounced, we were

reminded time and again, BYOO-duh. Byootiful Buda.

Dear St. Anthony …

But do I have the oomph to search for a relative? Or to do something if I found one? I don't think so. I just don't think so. Not now.

It's too late.

I'm too late.

20

I fiddled with an Internet search for a while but got no results. Well, millions of results but none that helped me. So today— yes, it's a new day but not "*a new day!*"

It feels a lot like yesterday and what, I imagine, tomorrow will feel like. Be like. Aren't I a "Little Miss Sunshine"?

Anyway, I'm leaving the jungle and returning to the forest. That is, from Vietnam to BWA. More than half a century ago. Fall 1966.

I've become a time traveler. An interesting thought. Probably be better if I remembered more of that BWA time so I could be more coherent here. Although, remembering more might make this even worse.

Not just the writing here but the reviewing of my years there. Only three, for God's sake, but every year packs more punch when you're young.

I suspect all of this—again, whatever it is or will become— is … . I have it. This is a quilt. "The Glory Bee Quilted Life of Jake Eastman." Patches and scraps.

"Bee" like a quilting bee, right? But, it seems to me, if you have to explain what you wrote then you didn't do a very good job writing it and/or it wasn't that clever, just stupid.

I really needddddddddddddddddddddddddddddddddddd

That's new. Suspended animation, I guess. Spaced out. Powered down. With my finger stuck on the D key. I'm back now. I'll leave it in because it, too, is a part of this story. (Let's just forget the quilt.)

Speaking of geometry—skipping a transition here. Time's short and the water's rising.

Speaking of geometry, I liked Mr. Heller. And I liked geometry. I'm trying to figure out now why his class was pleasant. I mean, it was still fifty minutes and those can drag on, but it wasn't, you know, biology. Or economics.

It's very hard to judge ages when time traveling. Mr. James Heller was *old*. Through fifteen-year-old eyes. And *young*. through sixty-eight-year-old eyes. (And trifocals.)

I'd guess early fifties.

A dark suit with chalk dust on the right sleeve. His board-writing and -erasing arm.

A little below average height, a little above average weight. Close-cropped hair. Gold wire-rim glasses. A completely uninhibited, unselfconscious, cornball sense of humor. Groaner puns and silly jokes.

A wooden pointer that still had a small black rubber pointed tip. Used on the board and, playfully, to smack a student on the shoulder.

A length of white string in his pants pocket that he would pull out and use as a compass and, along with a piece of chalk, draw circles and arcs—and, every once in a while, Mickey Mouse's head.

Squares and triangles and parallel lines and ... rhomboids? Wasn't that, I mean isn't that a geometry thing?

Except for slicing a pizza or a pie, who uses geometry? Besides mathematicians and engineers and carpenters and such. I mean, what real people use geometry in everyday life?

Huh. That last sentence. Who are "real people ?" And who

made me the judge?

I'm not *judging*, per se. (*That* sounds intelligent. I should use it more often.) I'm simply taking an honest look at BWA, my classmates, and the world of 1966.

For example:

21

Pudge and I were double *persona non grata*. Or, rather, double *personae non gratae*. Latin for "loser." Or "peasant" Or "dog sh*t."

(As if using an asterisk—or "star" as many say these days—somehow stopped anyone with even half a brain from knowing what the word is or what the writer meant. Certainly not "shot" or "shut.")

Here's why we two were so déclassé. Pudge was a Negro. A term then used at best. I had been, then was, and always would be poor white trash. And! We were both papists.

That is, *sniff*, Cath-o-lics. Not high church Anglicans but the real-deal indulgences and the Inquisition and Christ actually becomes a cookie (or, I suppose in England, a "biscuit") or a cookie becomes Christ.

How, what is the word?, cannibalistic if not ridiculous. Two words.

Look, I'm not the one to explain Catholic theology or dogma. Or to defend it beyond thinking, "Screw you, Catholic-haters. Just leave me alone."

The best person I knew, the one who in so many ways was closest to me and loved me in ways nobody else did, was an old Irish Catholic lady. An extremely kind and compassionate old Irish Catholic lady.

I wanted what she had and somehow being Cat-lick was a *huge* part of that.

It's funny. I mean weird. That I missed Dad and Grandma in such different ways. And, at the same time, in the same way.

Grief, the original cluster fu ... (Learned that expression from Dad. Still love it.)

What was I writing about? Just a sec.

Okay. At the end of the last section I wrote "For example:" and then today about how Pudge and I were ... . So today I wanted to write about going to Mass on Sunday. The two of us.

The three of us. Pudge, Murray, and me.

BWA had a non-resident chaplain who popped in on Sunday morning and led all the Prods. That is, Episcopalians, although—technically—members of the Church of England are not "Protestants." Prods, what?, descended from Luther and his ilk while Anglicans date back to Hank VIII.

Or not. I have no idea why I have that differentiation in my mind or if it's true.

I need to get to the point. But maybe my mental wanderings are the point. Maybe there's more than one point.

Maybe life is pointless.

Be that as it may ... Who used to say that? Ah, yes. The good headmaster, Dr. Bradshaw. What if he's at the reunion? That would really be something. How old would he be now?

I could just look online and find out if he's going to be an honored guest or some such.

Not *the* honored guest but still.

Headmaster Emeritus. Or Emeritus Headmaster?

Come to think of it, was he the one who said "be that as it may"?

Maybe not.

And maybe it doesn't matter if what I write is accurate but

the *value* of my writing this is my *writing this*. Journey not destination.

Wait. He died a while back. Did I already write that?

I can tell I need to stop for now.

22

I feel better today. A relative term but I'll take it.

I want to think about and write about going to Mass. My little bit of rebellion against the Orange Men. A term used here for those who know something about the historical relationship between Ireland and England. Grandma taught me some of this.

Not indoctrinating or railing, just telling family stories. About her family so about my family. Now how I wish I had listened more. Ah, well. I suspect no youngest generation listens as closely to the oldest generation as they wish they had when they become the oldest generation.

That's a horrible sentence. What I mean is I bet all my age-peers wish they had paid closer attention when Grandma or Grandpa was telling a story about (*yawn*) the old days or the old-old days of their own parents or grandparents.

Anyway ... .

Sunday morning services in the BWA chapel were mandatory for all students. And, yes, there was—and as far as I know still is—a real chapel. Brick building, pitched roof, timber-exposed ceiling, non-threatening (no saints beyond the apostles) stained glass windows, wooden pews, choir loft, altar … .

No tabernacle or votive candles, and no bingo cards (in a basement parish hall).

It seems pretty amazing that Pudge and I were the only Catholics among two hundred students. Maybe we weren't. I mean probably some guys were baptized (Catholic baptized) but not keen on going to Mass. Or on being Catholic.

Who knows? Not I. Ditto with any non-Christians. Agnostics. Atheists. And so on.

I'm also not clear on how it was Pudge and I got to leave the grounds and go to a neighboring Catholic church.

I draw a blank here. It must have been the first Sunday after the first day of school and there we were in Murray's car heading for St. Brendan's Church in the nearby suburb of Bothell. (St. Brendan himself being a sound sixth-century Irish fellah.)

Murray driving us in his 1957 Chevy Bel Air. I remember that. A make and model still much admired as a classic car.

I know we just called Murray "Murray" but I don't remember if that was his first or last name. If I ever knew.

No, it must have been his first name. All the BWA "help" were known by their first names.

Lou, Mel, Barney.

Or their nicknames.

Bobo, Jay, Chud.

Same with students by students: last name or nickname. If I go to the reunion I'm sure some of those boys from so long ago will call me "Carrie."

No one will refer to Pudge as "Lips." Bet my bottom dollar on that.

Anyway, to get back to my … what? … narrative. Murray was Filipino. We'd see him pretty often because one of his duties was cleaning profs' rooms.

Just now I just shuddered at the thought.

The entire student body and all the profs were in one four-story building. Kind of like a prison with inmates and live-in

guards.
> But not quite as pleasant.
> Focus, old man!

23

Getting out, a two-hour furlough, to go to weekly Mass would have been really great under different circumstances. The thing was, my circumstances were just so awful.

Here Grandma would have offered some "Yes, but at least … " statements pointing out how something worse would be, well, worse.

"Yes, I'm dead and your parents are dead but you've still got your health."

That was true. My physical health. Back then. My mental health, on the other hand, was a sack of … . I don't know what word or words to describe it.

A big sack. A full sack.

I'll say this about Holy Mother Church: the Mass is the Mass is the Mass. Each place on earth puts its own spin on some minor stuff but the main parts are the same.

In Bothell, Washington, or Bao Loc, Vietnam.

I bring this up because going to Mass on those Sundays in high school kind of tore me apart. Dissociation. I was back with Grandma on a Sunday or sometimes a weekday, too.

I was alone. In a pew surrounded by other people—nice people, good people, people who, as part of the Mass, were *literally* praying for me—but I was alone.

Pudge wasn't with his family but he had family.

Murray ... Geez, I don't know much about Murray. Short, wiry, old. Fifties? *Ha!* Maybe a family there. He sat with other Filipinos. A dozen or so. We sat with them. Sat, knelt, stood, walked up to Communion. Sang. Blessed ourselves.

They were very gracious, cordial, hospitable, welcoming to Pudge and me. The adults were. Kids are kids. But the kids were well behaved.

Wow. It just occurred to me I never associated them with Vietnamese people. At that time, my only image of any Vietnamese person was a man who killed Dad. Or men.

Or kid?

No specifics. I didn't let my mind wander down that trail. How the heck did I manage that? I have no idea.

Less than ten years later I could have easily, horribly, imagined all kinds of scenarios. I had seen them. Survived them. Unscathed except one small, pretty inconsequential wound that resulted in a couple of weeks in a hospital and then off to the States and a discharge. Plus a Purple Heart.

That—the medal—still upsets me. There were so many others who ... .

Dad ... .

Posthumously.

Dear God, I hate that word.

Something else. Okay.

"Hey, John, just how screwed up were you at St. Brendan's?"

Well, I was so screwed up I was in an all-boys boarding school and got to go where there were girls my own age once a week and I didn't pay any attention to them.

"Hey, John, are you gay?"

A fair question. No, I liked girls then and liked women when I got older.

"Hey, John, were you ever married?"

No. And to answer your likely next questions. I don't know why I never was. Dated some but never ...

"Hey, John, any kids?"
No kids. So no grandkids.
"Gee, John, did your whole life suck?"
No.
Or could be.
I don't know.
Maybe I'm writing this to find out.

24

I'm back. I needed to rest and then the day slipped into night. What was a saying? I mean before the Q. & A.

Just a second.

All right. I looked back at what I wrote yesterday Going to Mass. The three of us did that together for three school years. Till June of 1969. Graduation. Fifty years ago.

Golden class reunion.

No. Golden reunion, not a golden class.

Self-centered, mean-spirited, racist and classist, sons of ...

This isn't helping me.

I have to tell you—I have to tell *me?*—I don't want to see them again. To be with them. To listen to them.

Except, of course, for Pudge and Eric. Maybe we could just go get coffee. But I can't drink coffee now. All right, make mine tea.

Tea. Vietnam.

Shut up!

So—I assume—all but our tiny trinity are now fat cats who ... what? I don't know. I do know Eric and Pudge succeeded, too. But they were "good different" then so I'm sure they're "good different" now. At their core, they were just so decent.

We didn't know that back when we met and got to know each other over three years. Well, in a way we *did* know that back then but never would have used "at their core."

So we were what?

Decent, yes. Funny. Wise. And screwed. Wise *because* we were screwed.

Roll call!

Racism, grief/anger, and really crappy health. Like, you-may-not-live-till-you're-twenty type health.

(Yes, Grandma, you were right. I did have *my* health.)

Obviously, Eric reached twenty. And sixty-eight. Married, kids, and grandkids. Was handed the reins of the family fortune and took all members from incredibly rich to obscenely rich.

But still a nice guy. Like that fifteen-year-old kid.

Same for Pudge. Pudge, who … . Ah, Pudge.

And then there was John. Jake. Now there *is* John. Jake. Sitting here and … Stop, stop, stop!

Who wants to hear more about the fall of 1966? Better make that "the autumn of 1966." I've been saying "fall of 1966" a *lot*.

All right. Here we go.

Okay. Murray, Mass, girls, Filipinos. What else that first month? I know. "Visiting Sunday." That was when families could come out and visit with their sons.

This sounds like it's going to be really, really bad for me, right? Mom, dad, sibs. From one until four in the afternoon. Strolls around the campus. Most often some sort of food treat. A cake, a pie, a pizza. Something non-institutional. Anything non-institutional.

I'm going to guess it was the last Sunday in September, the first visiting day of the school year. I know that event was when I met Eric's and Pudge's families.

Shoot, I should say something about clothes. I'm pretty sure I mentioned our uniforms (and shiny shoes) but I didn't say I was given mine ("pre-owned") and it showed. Not new. Not a great fit.

That's not important here. Why go off track and ... ? I don't know.

I'm going to assume anyone my age writing about his or her life fifty years ago is going to be pretty much all over the place. It isn't just the "other stuff" that's mine alone. Probably all of them have "the stuff" that doesn't help.

Age and "other." A dual-threat scatterbrain.

I should make some notes and then do the writing. Great idea. Put them on a piece of scratch paper and then put that in a safe place and later have no idea where that safe place is.

This one is for you, Grandma: I don't have dementia and I'm very grateful for that. That, I think, would be worse. Really.

This might help with my writing: Tomorrow I'll talk about meeting Pudge's and Eric's moms.

God bless them. God rest their souls.

25

I think most of the families of first- and second-year students were at that Visiting Sunday. A term that really needs capital letters because it was A Big Deal. For the freshmen and sophomores. By eleventh- and twelfth-grade, not so much. The older guys just wanted the food.

So there might have been between one hundred and one hundred twenty-five families bopping around. That is, strolling sedately. Mothers and younger children properly dressed. Three-piece-suited fathers, in small clusters, busy with what we now refer to as "networking."

Gentlemen with the self-assured look of "We've got money and all's right with the world."

Pudge's family stood out. Surprise! But didn't look as if they felt out of place. They weren't out of place. Their son was a BWA student. Yes, it took a lawsuit but, well, he was in the right place now and so were they.

Mrs. Hudson brought a huge, homemade peach cobbler. Oh. My. God.

I would have loved her for that alone but even before I learned it was coming, she had touched my heart.

We were out in front the main building when Pudge began

introducing me. "Dad, Mom, this is ... "

But Mrs. Hudson wasn't waiting. She quickly stepped forward, facing me, and gave me a mom hug.

I don't remember any of those from my own mother but I'm sure that's what it was. Very similar to a grandma hug. I had had lots of those. But a mom hug ... .

So tight, so fierce , so tender.

And this whispered in my ear: "Oh, John, John, John."

She pulled back her head, still not letting go, and her eyes were shiny. "Oh, John." Then close again. When she finally released me and stepped back, Pudge and his dad and his sister and his two little brothers all had the same look on their faces.

"You're family now, John," Mr. Hudson said. "Mmm-hmm. You're family."

Mrs. Hudson wiped her eyes and said, "Shush."

Ignoring her, Mr. Hudson again said, "Mmm-hmm."

Oh, God help me, I started to cry. Big, fat, hot tears spilling down my cheeks. I was so embarrassed. Fifteen years old. Three years from becoming a soldier. Even now on a mission to be on a mission then.

When my breathing had returned to something closer to normal Pudge bumped the side of his shoulder into the side of mine and said, "You better like peach cobbler or you're out of the family."

26

I still do. Like peach cobbler. Love it. But none I've had since those years tasted like Mrs. Hudson's.

Okay, more about Pudges's family later but—trying to be organized here—I still have to tell you about meeting Eric's.

Same afternoon. What an afternoon.

Mr. and Mrs. Matthews.

Funny, I'm older now than both sets of parents were then but I still can't imagine called them Dan and Loretta or Bernie and Maxine.

So, Eric's parents were like Pudge's but not the same. Alike because very good, very accomplished, very caring people. Different because of race and economic backgrounds.

I never heard that one couple was the descendants of slaves and the other of slave owners but that seems very possible. Certainly the "descendants of slaves" part. One hundred and one years since the end of the civil war but ... .

So this is how I met Eric's parents and they met Pudge's.

Mrs. Hudson had dug around in her purse and handed me two tissues and I was blotting and blowing when Eric came up and—very formally—introduced Pudge and me to his parents. Then Pudge—very formally—introduced his parents to the Matthews.

Handshakes all around. Oh, and Mrs. Hudson pointed to and named Maria, Peter, and Paul. Pudge's twelve-year-old sister and his eight-year-old twin brothers.

The Matthews looked at my blotchy face and knew something was up. "Allergies," Eric said to his folks. "Plus, John's a little baby."

This from a guy who weighed, what?, half of what I did?

Mrs. Matthew took my left hand into her right hand and my right hand into her left hand. Sort of, I don't know, a WASP hug?

Understated compassion. Warm and very welcoming.

"Eric has told us about both of you," Mr. Matthews said, nodding to Pudge and me. "You three have established quite a bond in just a few weeks."

"United we stand," I said, surprising myself.

The four adults laughed … a little too loudly and little too long. Again, kindness. I was going to need more tissues.

"Marguerite made macaroons," Eric's mom said.

Alliteration," Pudge's sister said softly to herself.

"Cobbler," Peter or Paul said.

"Cookies," Paul or Peter said.

"Good lads," Mr. Matthews said. "Keep the meeting on topic. You'll go far."

"A little more alliteration?" Mrs. Matthews asked Maria. "Cobbler and cookies in an empty classroom?"

She nodded. The boys hopped.

As I write this I think it sounds really corny. Like a sappy movie or a goody-goody book for kids. But that's how I remember it, and what else do I have to go on?

How you remember things becomes your reality of the past.

I suppose I could ask someone who was there. All of that adult generation have passed away. And I haven't seen the kids who are no longer kids for … Wow. Must be decades.

We ended up in an empty classroom. The children—and teens!— pulled nine student desks into a circle and the ladies placed food, drinks, plates, and utensils on the teacher's desk.

Both moms were of the belief that said always bring a *lot* more than you think you'll need. And dear Marguerite, the Matthews' cook whom I would meet later that year, had surprised us all by including two quarts of vanilla ice cream. Packing it so it stayed (mostly) frozen.

Perfect for piling on cobbler and dipping with cookies.

I couldn't remember the last time I felt the way I did in that classroom with those people.

I started sniffing but didn't want to begin blotting.

"Allergies," Eric said to Pudge.

"And a little baby," Pudge answered.

"Boys!" both moms said.

"Teenagers," Mrs. Matthews said to Mrs. Hudson.

"May God have mercy on our souls," Mrs. Hudson answered.

27

And after that indoor picnic everything at BWA was just sugary sweet and fine and dandy. Yeah. Right.

They all packed up, said goodbye, and the three of us were still stuck there. No. It was where Pudge and Eric wanted to be. As much as any kid can want to be at school. Or, worse, at a boarding school.

I didn't want to be there. Even stuffed with treats and still warm from such a great afternoon, one little flame burned brighter. Hotter. The realization startled me. Frightened me. And, in a way I didn't understand, comforted me even as it goaded me.

Vietnam.

Them.

Him.

This is what the refectory—the dining hall—was like. I'm going to write about that now so I don't have to write about being eighteen, nineteen, and twenty.

So I don't have to think about it.

I'll just nip it. Nip it in the bud, as Deputy Barney Fife used to say. So did one of my mental health counselors. Not in those exact words but it was pretty much the message.

And it helped. Helps.

So in the BWA refectory, which—to plebeians—looked surprisingly like a dining hall, there were some twenty-five wooden rectangular tables with eight students at each. Two fourth-years, two third-, two second-, and two first-.

Yes, it sounds like the French concept of "Liberté, égalité, fraternité" (liberty, equality, fraternity) but for a Black kid and poor white kid there was little of any.

In theory the assigned seating was shuffled once a month. A new set of eight, but in the same order of four, three, two, one. Except not for Pudge and me. No matter how the cards were dealt—and to this day I have no idea who was in charge of that—Pudge and I were given the same hand.

Tablemates.

No sense sullying two tables, right? Little did the Seating Chart Nazi know he was doing us a favor. We liked being together. We wanted to be together. And, on rare months, Eric joined us.

That was really great.

I'm pretty sure I've mentioned Eric was held in low esteem because his family was such high society. Internationally loaded instead of Big Bucks in Nowhere Washington State.

I don't know if the Mathews' were billionaires back then. Probably not. Probably only hundreds of millions. But, I have no doubt, they are now.

Old money. *Noblesse oblige.* So rich they didn't have to be snooty. Have to put others down to bring themselves up (in their own eyes).

And as long as I'm on the topic. (Putting the refectory on hold, here.) At some point that fall I flat out asked Eric why his folks were so nice to me and Pudge and to Pudge's family.

He looked confused. As if it had never occurred to him to ask that question.

"This is going to sound braggy but I don't mean it that

way," he said.

"Okay."

"Dad travels a lot for work and often we all travel as a family. Including my older brother and sister."

I nodded.

"I mean Europe, Asia, Africa, South America." He shrugged.

"Not Australia?"

"Oh," he said. "Yeah. There, too, one time. Never Antarctica."

"Not yet," I said and he smiled.

"So what do your treks have to do with the Hudsons and me?"

"I think … I think … no, I'm sure. All of us have met a lot of people of different races and religions and ethnicities and nationalities … "

"Uh huh."

"And different economic circumstances," Eric said.

"Rich folk, poor folk."

"Really rich folk, really poor folk," he said.

"And … ?"

"Mom and Dad treat all of them with courtesy and respect." He paused. "Huh. I never stopped to ask why. It's just what they do so it's just what we do. I do."

"Even a Black kid and an Army brat."

"Those certainly put me to the test," he said. "I think I can hang on a little longer. No promises."

"Said the carrot-top boy."

"Blatant redhead-ism."

28

Maybe I shouldn't even pretend to try to make this chronological or stay on-topic. On-topics.

I could say more about the refectory. About the food, on the plates and on the walls.

I don't think good institutional food is possible. Even if it starts out okay, or even tasty, the sheer repetition of the menu items and lack of personal control makes it devolve into glop.

("Devolve"? Where they heck did that come from?)

Even with a buffet or salad bar. Choose what you want but the choices are predetermined.

At BWA and in the U.S. Army.

Profs and higher-ranking officers eat better. (Like kings, compared to students or grunts.) Maybe it has to do with a sense of entitlement. Of paying ones dues. Profs used to be lowly students. And even BWA alumni just scoffed at any complaints shared by present-day students, including their own sons.

"You guys have it so much better than back when ... "

Blah, blah, blah. With no sympathy for us now eating blah food.

In the Army you can start as a second lieutenant but you're

going to have to bump up several times to a better rank to get the really good chow. Not that I was ever in an officers' mess but I knew some guys who worked in them and they talked. (And, on more than one occasion, pilfered.)

Okay, that was on the plates at BWA but what about on the *walls*? And *ceiling*? (Boy, I am doing a bang-up job of staying on track today. "Good lad," Eric's dad would say.)

The refectory walls. I'll tell you—the unknown you—about the walls in the dining hall. I'll remind me —the me in some way trying to define me—about those walls.

It was a cavernous, high-ceilinged room so ... Wait!

First, the ceiling. Dotted with pats of butter flicked mid-meals by bored and brash adolescents who waited for those butter bombs to fall on some unsuspecting diner. (Not over the profs' table.)

Or to remain there for time immemorial as they oozed into a greasy stain.

Why did I interrupt to talk about this? I have no idea. But there it is.

So, as I was saying, the ceiling was high and so the walls were, too. By God, this makes for fascinating writing. And reading! The only question is who will play me in the movie. I recommend ... Well, I don't know the names of any actors who could play a fifteen-year-old. Walter Brennan could play the sixty-eight-year-old me except of course no one under sixty has ever heard of him. And he's been dead since 1974.

The latter isn't necessarily a problem. A body seated at a laptop and ... *action!* Or lack thereof.

Come on, Johnny boy, the walls. The walls, the walls, the walls don't mean much without the paintings.

There were half a dozen oil paintings on the walls Two on each except none behind the profs' dais.

High *and* mighty.

Two portraits—I don't know, maybe three feet by four feet in hoity-toity frames—of the august founders of Brookfield Washington Academy. Two alumni who had become fat cat (lard ass) donors. One alumnus who had snared a Nobel Prize in … something "sciencey." And one alumnus in uniform. U.S.M.C. A captain killed in the Battle of Peleliu.

Needless to say, his was my favorite even though he had been a gyrene. I developed the habit of giving him a small nod and a silent "Sir" when I entered or left the room.

Yes, a salute would have been much better but my life was already screwed up enough. "Have you seen, Eastman? He f**king salutes a picture."

Plus, when there was ever a blackout at dinner in winter months … I need to explain that. Not like some kind of "bombers have been spotted" blackout but when the joint briefly lost electricity. A blown fuse, downed wires from a windstorm, or some such.

Anyway. It was the custom—much disapproved of by the faculty—to use a spoon or fork to catapult food items at the six framed targets. When the lights came back on, *voila!*, bits of whatever had been on the dinner menu. Most of it hitting only the wall. Some of it scoring a direct hit on one of the six chaps.

On those occasions, I would linger after the meal and when the room was empty, clean off the captain's portrait.

My gosh, I haven't thought about that in years and years. I remember I was very serious about it and really honked off at the jerks who had made him a target.

Not the Japanese army. The jerks at BWA. It was like they had desecrated the grave of a military man. Like toilet-papering Arlington National Cemetery.

Dad was buried next to Mom, in Des Moines, with Grandma on the other side of her and then a grandpa I never met. Holy smokes, I might have the plot next to Dad. It seems to me Grandma said she bought a bunch after Grandpa died.

Huh.

29

I took yesterday off. A couple of visitors. Nice to see them. Usually they come on different days.

So it's not like I'm a hermit or anything.

Oh. Also, before I stop with refectory stuff, there's this: I haven't been to the school in almost fifty whole years but I am absolutely certain Pudge is on the wall now.

I hope students are flinging stuff at him. I know he would get a kick out of that.

Wow, maybe Eric, too. Not lobbing spaghetti noodles or anything like that but being the target of them. Yeah, I bet so. A few decades ago he bankrolled some new BWA building. Oh God, that.

Of course he invited Pudge and me to the dedication but neither one of us could make it. Work kept Pudge away and I … I don't do well with crowds. Or stress. Or a lot of other things.

Eric, being Eric, didn't hold it against us. Against me who had no real excuse. He mailed me a picture of "The Eastman Library."

There was also a handwritten note that said, "I hope this makes it to you. You know how mail carriers can be."

It made me smile.

His choice for the name of the building made me shake my head. I don't think I ever thanked him. Not then and not when we saw each other once or twice since then.

God, I'm a jerk.

Me, me, me.

I have to stop now. I really have to stop.

I'm back. A rest and a nap. A rest is if I lie down but don't sleep. A nap is if I'm resting and I fall asleep. Usually no dreams with a nap, just blessed dreamless sleep.

Holy crap!

The school library building is named for me so maybe students are throwing food-globs at my portrait, too. Nah. What could it be? A painting based on a yearbook photo? That would be grim.

I should tell you more about Mr. Stevenson. Sergeant Malcolm Stevens. Dad's buddy and my guardian. The guy who got me into BWA. Which, by the way, I don't hold against him. He saved my bacon. I was on the fast track to foster care. Even with all the rules and all the ... let's just say "students" ... I think I had more freedom at BWA.

And I'll (grudgingly) admit, the joint was rigorous academically. A3 was right.

So, about "Sarge." Like Dad, he fought in World War II, Korea, and Vietnam. He enlisted as soon as possible after the bombing of Pearl Harbor. Had his mom sign a permission slip to get in before he turned eighteen.

It took a while for me to learn those things about him. (Big surprise, right? The Tight-Lipped Generation.) He never used the word "mentor" and I'm sure Dad didn't either, but that's what he was to Dad. A sergeant who taught my father how to be a sergeant.

"He was a good man. He was a good soldier."

That wasn't just how Sarge summed up Dad, it was the

whole story. Yes, it said a lot but it would have been nice to hear a little more. A bunch more.

It occurs to me now that Dad's death must have touched Sarge deeply. And how close they were in age. Amazing what we don't think about, don't realize, as a teen ... or for much of our early- and middle-adult years.

What can seem so obvious later in life. Later in one's life.

My point here is Sarge (and Dad) considered himself a man when he was still a teen and so he figured I was, too. I suppose I could have gone to him if I had a problem but even as I write this now I know I wouldn't have. Well, I didn't.

Manhood. Freedom. Independence.

And Mrs. Hudson and Mrs. Mathews.

And Monica.

30

I've been thinking about her, too. Monica. Only met her once, about thirty years ago. I suppose she came to mind because I'm back getting Meals on Wheels.

Food delivered to me. A young woman—her name is Darinda—comes once a week and leaves me seven lunches and seven dinners. Frozen.

Monica wasn't a delivery person. She was the director and made a visit to my place to see if I liked the food and the service and if there were any problems.

I had been hurt at work, a (not-my-fault) car accident, and couldn't get around for about a month and half. I lived alone then. Now, too.

Anyway, she was just really nice. Kind. That's what she was. She was really kind.

I had never thought of her with Mrs. Hudson and Mrs. Matthews but they were all cut from the same cloth. Boy, that's an old expression. I don't know any new ones. The last "latest" one I can think of is "the new normal." I'm getting used to my "new normal" and, *shrug*, it's not like I have choice.

I think people used to say "that's just the way things are."

Now, "it is what it is." Wait. One more. "Suck it up, buttercup." I really like that one. Could have used that in Vietnam. A lot.

So, anyway, I just felt this connection with Monica but she had a wedding ring so … .

I hope her husband wasn't a jerk. Isn't a jerk. Some people have no idea how good they have it.

Did I have it good? I think so. Sometimes I did. This isn't supposed to be a boo-hoo memoir or something. Not a "pity party." Good for me! There's one more recent expression. Kind of recent. I guess.

I think I read somewhere, or someone told me, if you're writing some kind of autobiography or life review, the more you get into it the more you remember. Prime the pump.

There's an old expression. Even before my time.

I know I'm not "old old." Sixty-eight isn't "old old" because these days a lot of people make it into their eighties and even their nineties.

But my family's track record isn't so good. Holy smokes, I've already lived longer than any of them. As far as I know. I'm not sure about Dad's parents or any of their siblings. Grandma told me they were all gone but I didn't ask any more about it.

My gosh kids are stupid. No. That's not fair. Kids are kids. Always have been, always will be. And then they grow up. Or at least get older.

I suppose I should be grateful I have a chance to look back on, and sort of sort out, my life. ("Sort of sort out"?) Or at least sort through. I see it divided into these sections: Kid up until Dad and Grandma died. BWA. Army. Post office. Retirement. Now.

Army to post office. From one uniform to another. Most of my life was with the USPS. I had colleagues. Work buddies. But "friends"? I'll have to think about that.

The way to make a friend is be a friend. Well, that was (part of) my problem, wasn't it?

I think in all my life I had four friends. Really, really, good friends. Pudge, Eric, Dork, and Buddha. Two living, two dead.

I should go to the reunion.

Just suck it up, buttercup.

31

Regarding yesterday's final line: Today I add "or not." To just suck it up and go to the reunion. Or, at the very least, get in touch with Eric and find out when (if?) Pudge is coming to town and then meet with both of them.

Case closed. Except it sounds overwhelming. Something so simple. I could tell one of my weekly visitors about this and I'm pretty sure she'd offer to call Eric for me. Each would. The three ladies.

So I won't tell them. I think if I do this I want to do it on my own. To come to a final decision and take action by myself.

There's time. I still have a couple of months.

I don't want to think about the reunion today. I don't have to. Not today. I don't want to think about a couple of months from now.

Never put off till tomorrow what you can put off till many tomorrows after tomorrow. That's what I say.

So ... autobiography, memoir, life review. Probably good for me to do that. Do this. Let's see. In the year of Our Lord nineteen hundred and sixty-eight.

No. Let's make it 1966. That fall.

I'm trying to think of specific instances where it was obvious Pudge and I were outsiders. Much maligned (there's a word) by insiders. I should have a hundred examples right on the tip of my tongue.

Now that period seems, feels, more like an atmosphere. Gray. Oppressive. Suffocating.

Well, that's rather vague.

But you know, there may have been a part of the reason for it that wasn't BWA. Don't get me wrong. I mostly hated it there. But I had nowhere else to go. Nowhere else better. And there were some classmates other than Pudge and Eric who were okay.

So maybe part of my memories of that time also have a lot to do with Dad and Grandma. They were gone. Just gone. Dad KIA and Grandma an out-of-the-blue heart attack.

I don't know who found Dad or was with him when he was killed. Grandma was by herself and I came home and found her on the kitchen floor.

And I freaked out. The next thing I sort of remember is a neighbor lady was there and a police officer and some medics and ... .

That summer, and in so many ways that fall, is just a blur. Bits and pieces. Scraps. Grays, times, places, thoughts, events. Not big events like funerals. Those are really foggy. Some memories but it seems like I should have more.

Wouldn't a good son or grandson? I think so.

I skipped two lines here after that last paragraph because I had to spend a little time thinking about the last two sentences. A weird new thought. Maybe the fog, maybe the lack of memories, are because I *was* a good son and grandson.

I mean, I loved them and knew they loved me.

Maybe an ungrateful, unloving, jerk son or grandson would remember a lot more because he didn't really care. Or wasn't as affected.

That's sort of comforting.

Hey, John, only took you half a century to get there on this one!

Wait.

Dork and Buddha.

Privates First Class Baxter and McIntyre.

32

"Comrades in arms." *Ha!* That's what Dork—Baxter—used to call the three of us. It was so ... Dork.

And now seems ... so sweet.

Buddha—McIntyre—raised in a state not known for racial harmony would've given his life for ...

Did give his life for Dork, a soul brother—to use a term from that era— from the City of Brotherly Love.

Dork got hit. Buddha immediately crawled forward to pull him back to safety. Buddha got hit.

Two shots, two down, two gone.

And then there was one.

And now there is one.

I need to stop ... no, wait. My point when I started this was that time, the days, weeks, and months after those guys' deaths—after I had watched, heard, and smelled them die— was fog, too. Was blur.

Like the second half of 1966. Some memories but not many. Not as many, I suspect, as most people have. It's not that I'm losing my mind or my memory now. It's that those periods in my life just didn't ... record. A blank tape. A skip or series of skips.

That makes me feel better now. It's comforting.

I can remember the very first time I saw Pudge and Eric, and the very last time I saw Dork and Buddha alive. I have that. That's a lot.

Thank you for that, God. Thank you so much for that even though Vietnam still tears me apart. And, there's no doubt in my mind, always will.

It would be hard enough if it had been two soldiers I didn't even know. It's horrid because they were my friends.

My comrades.

All four—at BWA and in Vietnam—just boys. Like me, just a boy. How could I possibly know how to handle those events? Those times? Those emotions or lack of emotions?

From the news of Dad's death to my own returning to the States I did all right.

I really did.

Because I didn't just get from "there to there." *Poof!* I got *through* that time period. All of it. Every stupid, stinking, terrifying, hellish, heart-breaking day. Night. Moment.

I did that. With help, without a doubt. But I did that.

Beginning it as a boy and completing it as a man.

A young man, yes, but a man.

All that by the time I was twenty. Old enough to vote because of recent changes in the law but too young to drink in many states. Legally drink.

Home from the war but without a home. What did I do? Let me think.

Fort Lewis, south of Seattle. A lot of what now would be called exit interviews. In many different forms and with many different forms. Pretty much, "Yeah, you're fine, see ya."

Off the base, a car for sale. Always a lot of stuff for sale just off any military base. Blue. A 1963 VW squareback. Like a little station wagon. I remember thinking *I can fold down the back seat and sleep in there.*

I was wrong.

Five hundred dollars. Must have been some paperwork.

Hop on Interstate 5 and head north. Through Tacoma, through Seattle, into Everett. Sick of the freeway, hang a right, some lefts, some more rights.

Sleepy little town butting up against the foothills. The Cascade Range.

Car sputters and dies.

Fold down the back seat and there's no way I can sleep there.

Walk toward café, see "For Rent" sign on small house down a side street.

Half an hour later I have a house, if not a home.

How the heck did I remember all that? Really. How?

I have no idea.

33

I could speculate that I remember those details because it was my first day out of the Army, my first car, and my first home of my own.

Maybe. Or maybe because it was the first time in a long, long time that I was out in the open and not overly concerned about someone shooting at me or firing a mortar in my direction.

Not *overly* concerned. But by no means relaxed.

Anyway, through the grace of God/dumb luck I avoided a lot of the antagonistic behavior way too many Vietnam vets had to face. (Yeah, just exactly what they needed. Like it was all their fault and not some fat-cat white men and gutless presidents.)

So that was how I ended up in Granite Falls, population less than a thousand. Proud-to-be Americans who didn't take kindly to hippies, Commies, or draft-dodgers.

Home Sweet Home.

The car was okay. I had run out of gas.

Fortunately, I had enough money squirreled away not just to buy the car and rent the house, but take my time looking for a job.

Before I had ever heard the term, I was on a "sabbatical."

And, though not on the prowl, I met a really nice girl. Two years younger than I was. A recent graduate of the local high school and now working at the café. Not a waitress, a short order cook. Blonde hair held back with a blue bandana. Light blue eyes. Truly lovely face.

I could add nice shoulders and strong, sinewy arms because that was all I could see of her over the next five days when I showed up for breakfast each morning at six-thirty.

She'd set a plate of food on the shelf of a glassless, rectangular window between the kitchen and dining room—there must be a name for that—and say, "Order up." Not shouting but clearly heard.

All this was behind a counter that had stools. About a dozen of them. I sat in the main part of the room at one of a few tables for two. There were some for four. No booths.

A typical small café. A typical small diner.

The lone waitress looked like an older version of the cook. And, I later learned, she was. Her mom. A family-owned place run by the two of them and the mom's mom.

Her dad, the girl's, had left them when she was in grade school. Again, I knew nothing of that during my first week's patronage. Bit by bit (bite by bite?), she—Marilyn—told me about it.

At first I thought she was kind of snobbish but she was shy. Really shy. And I, no surprise here, knew just about nothing of dating.

Not a lot of the girls who buzzed around BWA wanted to have anything to do with me. The poor orphan was not a catch, even for going to a movie or school dance or whatever else it was other students did.

"Orphan." I don't know if back then I ever used that word to describe myself. I don't think so because even writing it here surprises me.

I was, of course.

Fifteen and no parents. No family. I had the proper

credentials, all right.
But about Marilyn.

34

The thing about falling for a girl when you're a twenty-year-old combat veteran is that it sounds ridiculous to call it "puppy love."

I think that's what it was for both of us, although I'm pretty sure puppy love can evolve into a more mature love. Maybe, early on, that's what both of us, and her mom, hoped would happen.

There is this: we gave it our best shot.

I'm not saying I hadn't been with other girls—considering what's just outside Army bases—but that had nothing to do with love.

This did. I'm sure of that and I still fantasize about what my life would have been like if I'd settled down there, married Marilyn, and raised a family. A real home. Grandkids.

That would have been nice. That would have been really nice.

But, how to put this, we were both pretty screwed up because of our backgrounds. No. That's not right. She was a little off-kilter at the time we met and I was really screwed up.

I think she knew that about herself and so she was in no rush to marry and settle down. And, now I strongly suspect, she knew the truth about me, too.

A nice guy. A good guy. But—as it's described these days—"with issues."

Huh. Another brand new thought:

If we had gotten serious, gotten married and started a family, I might have shattered the whole thing. I, like her dad, might have just upped and left. Never to return. Never a word.

Maybe the best thing she ever did for herself was end it with me. That took maturity. Courage. Wisdom.

And, in a way, she did it *for* me. Because of her I wasn't the guy who walked away. I don't want to be that guy.

A second new thought:

Parts of my life have been very hard but I don't think I ever hurt anyone that way. Not a wife. Not children. That … that would have been worse than all the time I've spent alone.

I'm pretty sure, one way or another, I would have ended up by myself. But I'm feeling great comfort in the fact I didn't leave destruction in my wake.

That's something for a headstone: "He could have been much, much worse."

Okay, more on Granite Falls. No. First about money.

I had a bunch of it back then. I had saved a lot of my pay, although my pay wasn't a lot. And I was Dad's life insurance beneficiary.

And, later in 1967, Grandma's estate—such as it was— was settled and the money came to me.

During that short time between Dad's death and her own, Grandma had been my guardian so she took care of all that needed to be taken care of with that. And then Sarge was.

No, he didn't steal it or anything like that. He just didn't dole it out willy-nilly to some dumb teenager.

Boy, you don't hear that much anymore, do you? "Willy-nilly." That's a good word. I hope it makes a comeback.

So I had a sizable chunk of change when I entered BWA, when I left BWA, when I entered the Army, and when I left the Army. (And we mustn't forget my shine-those-shoes income in high school.)

Grandma had lived through the Depression. Dad had been a child of it. Their attitude toward savings became mine.

Not cheap, just penny-pinching frugal.

Okay. I'm glad I remembered to include that in this life recap.

I've never been rich but I've never been poor. I chalk that up as a win.

35

I just reread what I wrote a few days ago. About Granite Falls and life insurance and an estate and all that. This project's been on hold for a little while because I needed a bit of a break.

I'm okay.

So anyway, Marilyn—the Belle of Snohomish County—and I got engaged ... Wait. I already told you it didn't work out, right? I think I did.

It didn't work out for us. I mean it didn't right then but in the long run it did. Not for "us" but for "her" and for "me."

Let me think. It was right after I was discharged that I rented the house. A few months earlier she had graduated and then she went to a community college in Everett for a year and I worked up in the woods.

Lumberman. It was just what I needed. Hard, demanding, dangerous, unforgiving, merciless ... . Everyday there were ten ways to get killed or maimed but, on the bright side, it wasn't combat in Vietnam.

I had a good foreman. Boy, that's rare. At the post office there were ... No. I'll save that for later.

So Marilyn was commuting to school and working at the

diner and living with her mom. I was in my house and in the woods and in the diner when Marilyn was working.

The foreman—what the heck was his name?—was old. To me then. Probably early fifties. A wife and four grown kids. Three young grandkids.

He and his wife—Cheryl—well shoot, I can remember her name but not his. Cheryl a-a-a-a-a-nd … nope. Anyway, they had a two-bedroom cabin up on some property deep in the woods.

Now it would be described as "off the grid."

He had built it. She had made it a home away from home.

So that first summer I was in "Granite" he had hired me a little before …

No. Wait. I took some time off that first summer after I got out. It was the second summer. That's right. The first summer I was in town and, let me tell you, those small towns like to blow the crap out of stuff for the Fourth of July.

It wasn't just the boys that were doing that. It was the dads, too. Probably some granddads.

Get all kinds of ordnance from the nearest Indian reservation, take it home, and *boom-boom-BOOM!*

For days and nights.

I stayed inside. Hid inside. Something stuffed in my ears to muffle the sound. God, it was just … .

I have no idea why I didn't simply get in my car and drive away. It seems like such a logical and simple solution. It *never* occurred to me.

I have to stop. I can't write about this. Stop. Stop, stop, stop.

Stop, John. Just stop. Just. Stop.

36

Same place. Different day. I don't know who invented, no, discovered some of the meds I take but God bless them. Dear God, bless those men and women.

I'll jump ahead. The next summer Cheryl and Jim—got it!—had me up at their cabin for a week that included the Fourth of July.

So quiet. So peaceful. Except for the playful banter between them as they blazed through hand after hand of gin rummy.

I walked in the woods. Ate a lot. (Lord, that woman could cook!) Slept. And read. I'd say the shelves of the cabin's huge bookshelf groaned under the weight of all the books available there but Jim built the bookshelf.

It was *solid.*

So were the two of them.

They treated me like a son. A grown son but one of theirs.

Like Pudge's folks had. I never thought of that. And Eric's.

I think the moms had a lot to do with that—what with me losing my own mother when I was three—but the dads were all-in, too.

My God, people can be so, so good. So generous with kindness. What a difference that makes in one's lifetime. Whether giving or receiving.

By the time the next Fourth rolled around I had moved on. Into Seattle. New job. New, sort of, career. No, it was. A career. Thirty years at it.

A couple of things. I need to backtrack.

The bright lights of Everett (county seat and then with a population of about fifty thousand) helped lure Marilyn from Granite Falls.

That and some guy who lived in nearby Marysville and went to Everett Community College.

Oh, those college boy classmates! I never stood a chance.

As I've said, it was all for the best.

Jim gave me a bit of a kick in the pants, too. I don't remember his exact words but the message was this: "I'd never fire you because you're a hell of worker and a hell of a good guy but you need to get the hell out of Granite and on with your life."

Did I mention he said "hell" a lot?

"Resting up was a good idea," he said. "Wise for a fellah your age. Now give it a try out there. See what you think. If you change your mind, you're always welcome here."

He'd noticed I had become restless. Especially after Marilyn gave me a "it's not me, it's you" speech.

She was right. It was me.

So we, Jim and I, talked about some possibilities and then I applied for a job with the post office. "Pension" was another word he said a lot.

So I sent in my application, got accepted, said goodbye to Granite Falls and its citizens, and headed south to Seattle.

Shoot, no, wait. One more thing.

I had said goodbye to Jim earlier and he wasn't with Cheryl the last time I saw her. Inspired by Grandma/the Holy Spirit, I thanked her again for that week at the cabin.

She gave me a sad, little smile. "Jim was so glad you came," she said. "We go up every year during the Fourth."

I nodded.

"No," she said. "I don't think you understand. He and my father built the place in 1947."

"So it wasn't just him?" I asked.

"Mostly. But Dad helped. He was the instigator. Gave us the land."

I still didn't get it. She took my hands in hers and gently squeezed.

"Dad was in Belleau Wood. Jim in the Battle of the Bulge. My younger brother, Peter, was killed in action outside a village in Korea you've never heard of."

Her eyes were moist.

"What about your boys?" I asked, afraid.

"Asthma." That little smile. And then:

"Peace, John. That's my prayer for you. Peace here." She lightly tapped my chest. "And here." She did the same to my forehead.

It was the greatest, the most powerful, the most needed, blessing I would ever receive.

37

Well, I'm all out of whack here. I need to get back to BWA. Eek! Back to BWA, saints preserve us! (Grandma.)

I mean I jumped way ahead in my timeline, my lifeline, and I need to get back to my first semester at Brookfield Washington Academy.

Okay, there was Visiting Sunday and Pudge's and Eric's parents and then … ? What then?

Classes? Ugh. Wrote about those. Sports? Nah. More than already covered. Classmates? Ick.

No, that's not fair. Let me dredge up some good guys. There were good guys. Not just Pudge and Eric. The challenge here is the jerks stink up the whole experience to such a degree it's easy to overlook the good guys.

"How was the soup, sir?"

"Well, except for the hair [cockroach, rat turds], it was first rate."

So I will try to focus on the soup and not the hairs, cockroaches, or turds.

I should just ask Eric for a class list. I know he'd have it because he'd have his annuals.

Okay. Time out. I'll be back.

Same-day-service.

I sent him an email and he wrote right back. He must have my name on some cut-through-the crap list.

I'm touched.

And just like that, here's the list. Highly likely one of his assistants put it together but the return message is all his.

"Jake! I bet these guys are old now. Like 'Mothballs.' Remember him? American history prof. Third Year. Oh, dear. He was probably only about fifty. 'Only'? Uh oh.

"I'll send more info later.

"Come to the reunion! We'll laugh at Pudge's style in hats.

"Eric

"P.S. My hair is no longer red. The little I have left is kind of brownish, tannish, I-don't-know-whatish."

When had we last seen each other? Let me think.

Maybe I already wrote about this. My mind gets foggy sometimes. More foggy. In general I feel as if I'm not thinking as clearly as I did when I was younger. Younger being ten years ago. Younger being before I got sick.

Enough of that. So ... .

Let me see if I can come up with an Eric story. He was really bright. Like Pudge. I was no academic slouch but those guys were something!

Most of our BWA classmates were bright. The book learnin' *was* pretty "rigris" so there was a weeding out of those who couldn't cut it. Some left on their own. Some had it suggested to them, and their parents, that they probably should leave. Some got expelled, and some of those because they wanted to be expelled.

Eric. An Eric story.

He was smaller than us. I mean Pudge, me, and our classmates. He might have been the smallest guy in the school that first year I was there.

Funny. I haven't thought about that in decades because I didn't think about it when all three of us were fifteen.

That's really strange. Pudge and I didn't tease him about it and I don't remember anyone else doing it either.

Yeah, the family was richer than God and all that, but did it really keep others from ragging him about his size?

Hmm. Maybe it was because he was such a nice guy to everybody. Not a doormat or anything but just ... .

Decent.

A good guy.

I mean the others were on him about a lot of different stuff but never his size.

That's weird. Why would that be? I'd like to ask him and Pudge. Get their theories.

God, I miss those two guys. I miss being fifteen with them. They're on my unwritten list of "People Who Saved My Life."

38

I woke up this morning thinking about Grandma McCarthy. Well, thinking about how I had to go to the bathroom and about Grandma.

I don't think I've included her last name in this. When I was a kid grandparents went by their last names. These days I suppose it'd be "Grandma Rose."

She was amazing. I remember Dad teasing her and saying her name should be McArthur, her being such a little general when it came to running things.

To which she would reply: "Button it up, Sergeant."

"Ma'am, yes, ma'am." Snapping to attention.

Both of them were big on me following rules but in a good way. And they had a unique relationship.

New thought: I bet a big part of that was because the dear young lady they had loved so much was no longer there. Each grieved, each suffered, in his or her own way.

Neither knowing how soon they'd be with Mom in heaven.

They're lucky. You have to reach a certain age before you realize the dead ones are the lucky ones. Maybe people who don't believe in an afterlife don't see it that way. Or not as easily.

When did I become so philosophical? Or is it theological?

Grandma. I was saying I woke up thinking about her. Remembering her. Now doing that doesn't hurt the way it did in fall 1966.

Such a weird time. Looking back it seems I was in constant pain and constantly numb. I don't know how that could be.

But there it was.

I did have moment, pockets, of relief if not joy. Again, Pudge and Eric. Wiser than their years.

Focus, John! About Grandma.

So why don't I want to see them at the reunion? Come on, man. Fifty years. I do and I don't.

My first thought: They're successes. I'm not. That sounds cold but I think it's true. What they did with their lives and here I am with mine. Down to a one-bedroom condominium in North Seattle. A small one-bedroom.

Their resumes, their *curriculum vitae*, their accomplishments.

I think the three of us were peers, or kind of peers, when we parted company in June 1969 but maybe not. Not really.

Why not?

Two young men heading for college and graduate school and beyond.

One young man walking into a jungle.

One, it seems like sometimes, who never really got out of that jungle. Never escaped. Or escaped with a part of him missing. Multiple parts. Each important for living a life that's … I don't know. Full.

What if I had just died there? In those few seconds between Buddha and Dork?

Three shots. Three down.

Three shots … . Three down … .

I need to take a break here.

39

I feel better. Relatively speaking. I'm not sure how to describe what happens. Revved up on a troublesome—horrific—thought or memory and then the speed, the intensity, just keeps increasing.

With me just sitting there. Or lying there. Or curled up there.

It's not like it was when I was younger. The grief, after Dad and Grandma died. The ... other stuff ... after ... the other stuff in Vietnam.

My mind is like a car that's okay most of the time, or at least a lot of the time, but then the accelerator gets stuck and it just races and races and races.

With the transmission in park.

Therapy, meds, coping strategies. It's been a long, long trail a-winding.

One that's winding down.

Complete confession. Total disclosure. What's the term used these days? Full transparency. Not baring my soul but saying something about my body which, I strongly suspect, has been readily apparent from what I've already written.

Knock, knock.

Who's there?
Death.
Death who?
Death who's comin' for to carry you ho-o-ome.

Well, it only took me forty days of writing this to get to the point. That being, my being is soon coming to an end.

My life on earth. What's *after* that? Nobody knows for sure. Nobody who isn't dead. But I think there's a heaven and, as a lot of combat vets have noted, "I've already spent my time in hell."

Boy, ain't that the truth.

So, the Meals on Wheels lady who visits me here now is— I don't want to say "just the Meals on Wheels lady" because she's more than that. Really quite wonderful to me.

The other two weekly visitors are a hospice nurse and a hospice social worker. They, too, are wonderful.

It was the social worker who floated the idea of me writing some stuff down. I wasn't what you'd call receptive. I thought I could pretty much sum up my life in a haiku.

Remember those? A traditional Japanese form of poetry. Three lines. Seventeen syllables: 5/7/5.

Question: Did WWII vets who fought in the Pacific say "screw that" when someone told them about haikus. Maybe in a college class, courtesy of the G.I. bill.

I bet not. I bet they didn't say "screw."

What if it were a traditional *Vietnamese* form? Ooh. I don't know. I can tell you I've never been to a Vietnamese restaurant since I got back to the States. But, here's one for you (or, I suppose, for me): I've been to a Vietnamese backyard barbecue in Seattle.

Hamburgers, hot dogs, potato salad, chocolate chip cookies.

U.S.A.!

And rice and fish and other menu items, I don't know the names of, from the old country.

It was back when I had a two-bedroom house. I lived

there for thirty years. Moved here to the condo about, oh, eighteen months after I'd retired from the post office at age fifty-five.

Wait. I never said what I'm dying from. Or, put more bluntly, what's killing me.

Oh, I don't want to. You know? All that rigmarole with early troubles and doctor appointments and then a specialist and the diagnosis confirmed and ... Oh, God, I really don't want to go back over all that here.

Hey!

I don't have to.

Screw transparency. Maybe not using the word "screw."

Let's get back to the picnic.

40

Yes, today about the picnic but after I finished writing yesterday I did some rummaging around in my stuff and found this:

A child of hopes and promises.
A teen too young too old.
A broken man, dream, life.

That doesn't follow the 5/7/5 scheme for syllables. Apparently the best I could do a while back when I learned I had ...

Oh, well.

A new day, a new ... what? Do not ask for whom the clock ticks. It ticks for thee. Except who has a ticking clock these days? Or a wristwatch that doesn't run on a battery? Or a wristwatch period?

If you have a bell tolling for you it's probably just your phone's ringtone.

It seems pretty clear I'm not in a picnic mood. Or in a mood to write about a long-ago picnic. "I am the ghost of picnic past."

I swear, it seems my mind has only two gears: race or bounce around. No. There's another: sadness. One more: fear. Of the unknown.

Faith can take a lot of presuming and assuming. I suppose if it didn't, it wouldn't be faith. What would it be?

Blessed assurance, like in the old hymn? I suppose but I suppose, also, for most people that's what their mom offered them. A caress, a "shush now, you're going to be all right."

I bet I had that from my mother but I don't remember it. Maybe no kid, now an adult, remembers the particular times and circumstances. It's deeper than that. Forgotten but never forgotten.

Maybe I was too little. She died too soon.

I didn't get that form of comforting from Dad. Not motherly but like a dad and a widower and a sergeant in the U.S. Army.

Not brusque or unkind or unfeeling, just different. Maybe all dads do that differently than all moms.

But Grandma must have done it. So there must be some of it, echoes of it, in me.

Sometimes I still fold my arms across my chest and rub my upper arms and kind of twist side to side a little and softly say, "Shush now, you're going to be all right."

Oh, God. I give myself a hug. I never thought of it that way.

Oh crap, now I'm starting to cry.

We should have gone to the picnic. You and I. Or I and I.

Okay. Deep breaths. Nice and slow. In through the nose, hold it, and out through the mouth.

What would you do if you had only X many days to live?

Well, I'd do this and that and the other and different stuff and my bucket list and then that and this and …

Maybe you would. Apparently I'm not.

I do have a goal though. I would really, really like to die in my condo. Is that asking too much, God? Come on. Give me that. I'll be your friend.

Forever.

God's will. God's plan.

Well, here's something for you, God, to consider, you Omnipotent and Omniscient Being: nobody likes a know-it-all.

Just sayin'.

It's good to smile. It's good to tease the Creator of all that is, was, or ever will be.

Wow, I hope you have a good sense of humor.

Come on, Big Guy, lighten' up.

And I will, too.

Thus endeth midday prayers, traditionally in the Liturgy of the Hours called "Sext."

Midday sexting. I strongly suggest the Church renames it.

That's enough for today.

Over and out. Same time, same place, tomorrow.

Huh, Lord? Huh?

Or not.

"Or not" would be okay.

41

Well, look who's back at it on a brand-spanking-new day.

Here I am, Lord. I come to say "what the heck?"

Ooh. Maybe I died and this is hell. Not combat hell, just—I don't know— "North Seattle hell"? *Ha!* That would have to include being stuck in traffic.

Some guy, a philosopher or such, said "hell is other people." What if you're stuck with yourself? What if *you* are hell for *yourself?*

What the hell!

I'm just goofing around here. I must be feeling better if I can goof. *Goofing with God.* My next book. Not that I have a first book.

Wait. *This* is my first book. Huh. Well, isn't that something? I'm writing a book. Who would have guessed it? Not I.

Just a second.

Okay, I'm back. A little clicking on the computer. More than twenty thousand words written and I'm still cranking right along. Author-wise. Health-wise is another story. That's a part of this story. Wow, maybe I'm not just a writer, I'm a philosopher, too.

Coming from the Greek for "lover of wisdom."

"Yo, baby, I'm not a fighter, I'm a lover of wisdom."

I have to ask the nurse if some new side effect of one of my meds has kicked in. Really. Yesterday's writing and this. Whoa.

Not that it matters. I'll take it. The meds and the new side effect. I like it.

How you doing, John?

Well, I don't have long to live but right now is really, really good.

Here's something that I really, really hate. (To change the subject a bit and use "really, really" too close together. Really.)

I hate it when someone kind of shrugs off another person's terminal diagnosis and says, "Well, we're *all* dying."

Kiss my big, fat, terminally ill ...

I mean I know some people are trying to be upbeat and some are just obtuse but one way or the other ... just don't.

There. My third book: *John Eastman's Tips from the Dying.*

Maybe a subtitle: *How to Avoid Sticking Your Foot in Your Mouth or Behaving Like You Have Your Head Up Your ...*

Here's a preview from the "What to Say" chapter: "Oh, man, that sucks." "I'm so sorry." "You're in my prayers." Or "in my thoughts." Or "I'm sending good energy your way." Or whatever floats your existential boat.

I'm being kind of harsh here. *Mea culpa.* ("O my God, I am ~~hardly~~ heartily sorry ... .")

People who have never been around death and the dying have a hard time being around death and the dying. It's not their fault. They just never learned. Never had to learn. Sometimes ignorance *is* bliss.

But let me just add—*My, my, my. Who woke up being Mr. Bossy this morning? Raise your hand, John.*—it can be a good idea to learn something about ways to behave in that situation. What to say. What not to say. What helps and what doesn't.

You know, I think I'm way off track here. How did my

life review turn into some kind of snippy how-to? Into stern admonishment.

Look. If at times in your life you've found yourself chin-deep in poop then you have an idea of what it's like for someone else who now finds himself or herself chin-deep in poop.

If it's never happened to you, do a little research on poop.

That's all.

And for today, that is all.

Nap time.

42

Sometime I wake up and then I remember I'm dying.

That's what happened this morning. Not the cheeriest way to start the day but there was no physical pain. So I'll take it.

I don't want to write about death. Or pain. And I don't have to.

Pre-Thanksgiving 1966.

Let me tell you about that.

I wasn't sure what I was going to do for the holiday and just the thought of it made my fists clench as my stomach tightened.

In prior years, most often it was Mass with Grandma and then back home and people from the neighborhood and parish coming and … .

Ah, you know. Aromas, laughter, food, TV football. Not Norman Rockwell but not Norman Bates.

Hey, I'm getting better at this writing stuff.

Pudge's mom sent me a letter in mid-October inviting me to join them and go down to Portland for an extended-family gathering there.

Leave Wednesday, back Friday.

It sounded like too much. It sounded impossible.

I wrote her back and thanked her but said I had other plans. I didn't. Well, I did. I planned on doing something else but I didn't know what that something else was. Yet.

I read my response letter to Pudge and asked him if it sounded okay. Not rude or anything.

"You're fine," he said. "Mom told me whatever you decide to do to get through this Thanksgiving is what you should do."

"Oh." I was relieved.

"Plus," he added, "none of us really like you."

I had been to their house twice. For dinner.

"I think your sister kind of does," I said.

"Shut up."

"Okay."

"I mean it," he said.

"Okay."

"She's only twelve!" Then he saw the look on my face. *Gotcha!* "You jerk," he said.

"It's only three years' difference."

"Jerk."

No, it wasn't two dinners. It was one dinner and one lunch. I suppose that doesn't matter.

In early October and early November BWA students got to go home for a day. Not overnight. Both times I went with Pudge and it was ... foreign.

Different. But good different. Nice different.

Part of that was their being a Black family. I don't mean that in a negative way. Anything but. It would have been like Pudge going to some big Irish family shindig.

The basics are the same, the details are different.

Plus, with Pudge, there were more kids. His sister and two brothers.

No grandma living there.

But a mom.

That was the big difference. A really wonderful thing that

made me sad. Inside. But I did a good job of hiding that. Both times.

Wait. I have that wrong. No, I didn't do a good job of hiding it. I bet both of Pudge's parents saw that.

They were sharp. Really sharp.

Memory: At my first meal there, the lunch, his dad asked me how I was settling in at BWA. Any troubles.

"One," I said and both he and Pudge's mom kind of leaned in. I waited a beat and then said, "I would really like a new roommate."

Rim shot! Thank you very much!

An appreciative audience.

"Well, that goes without saying," Mr. Hudson said. "You can see why his mother and I worked so hard to get him out of the house."

"Took it to court," I said.

"No stone left unturned."

Mrs. Hudson reached over and gave my hand a squeeze.

A "squeeze."

Kind of like Cheryl would, up in Granite Falls.

Huh.

They were a lot alike. That's interesting.

For dessert Pudge's sister Maria had made a two-layer Miracle Whip chocolate cake with fudge frosting. She gave me a large slice.

I remember noticing Maria had brown eyes like Pudge's but they looked a lot better on her.

43

I called the Des Moines cemetery this morning. No, not to confirm my reservation.

I was wondering how old Grandma was when Grandpa died. When did she become a widow compared to Dad becoming a widower?

(And, yes, I've been getting into the habit of reading the obituaries in the newspaper every day. Online.)

So here's what I found out.

No. I don't want to think about it. About them. I'll come back to this. Maybe. Not today. Not now. I want to run away. That's what I want for now.

Just be somewhere else. Maybe just be *someone* else. But I don't know who. Of all the people I've met over the last sixty-eight years there's no one I want to be other than me.

Okay, I'll try this again. I'll see if I can just distract myself. Not think by thinking about something else.

I never did tell you about Thanksgiving 1966, did I? I said Pudge's family was going to Portland and that was beyond my capabilities. It was too much.

I think I'm repeating myself here. I can't focus. I can't get into this even with a running start. Or a crawling start.

Into what?

Into today's chapter of *My Life Review.*

Let's see.

About a week before the Thanksgiving break the building lost electricity during dinner and the food went flying toward the portraits on the refectory walls. I told you how that would happen, right?

Teenage boys, no respect. Noodles dangling from the images of BWA's august forefathers when the lights popped back on.

I guess I really don't want to write about, think about, Grandma and Grandpa. About Mom and Dad. Four headstones, five plots. One with a reserved sign.

Maybe, at this point, it doesn't matter what year each of them was born. Or died. I mean, they've all been gone a long, long time.

Not so, of course, for Dad and Grandma then, in November 1966. It hadn't been a long time. Only months.

Eric's parents invited me to spend the holiday with them. The holiday weekend Wednesday afternoon through Sunday evening. Back at BWA by eight.

I remember. Mrs. Matthews sent me a letter. (Thick stationery. Monogramed.)

That's right. She asked me to do her a favor and spend the time with them. Eric had an older brother and sister but neither was going to be able to make it home.

Mrs. Matthews would so appreciate my keeping her and the others company. She would make sure I could get to Mass on Sunday morning and did I have a particular dish I would like for Thanksgiving dinner?

I showed the letter to Eric and Pudge.

"You should go," Pudge said. "You're not much but ... I

don't know. Apparently better than nothing."

"Little bit," Eric agreed.

"Come on," Pudge said. "You can tell me how Eric's family just barely scrapes by. Living hand to mouth."

Eric looked at Pudge, turned his back, and then said to me: "You can have the entire third floor, if you like."

44

He wasn't kidding. And it wasn't the house's top floor.

I had never been in a mansion. It was astounding. The swankiest in a really swanky Seattle neighborhood. I could have used a map just to get around inside.

I suppose I should know the square footage, number of rooms (number of bedrooms and bathrooms) and on and on and on, but here's my strongest memory:

It was a home.

It was warm and inviting because its residents were warm and inviting. Like Pudge's family and their house. So different but so the same.

It was hard not to envy both families. Impossible.

What's the deal, God? Explain it to me. Why did they get *that* but I got … . A harder life. You know that's true.

And, odds are, Pudge and Eric will get a longer life.

Yeah, yeah, yeah, we never know but … . I'm pretty sure they aren't in hospice.

Here's the good part: I get to remeet Mom. "Mommy." That was probably how I addressed her when I was three. Maybe "Mama" when I was even younger.

Three years old, God! Just three years.

Oh, but all eternity with her after I croak. Yeah, well, and a lot of years without her here. The vast majority of my childhood and all my teenage years and maybe I wouldn't have gone to Vietnam if you—Mama—had been alive and you would have said, "Oh, please don't do that" and then I would have been mad at you and …

I don't know. I think my life would have been a lot better. I know it. It would have been like other kids' lives. Not perfect but … .

I still feel anger. Not at you, Mom. It wasn't your fault. Grandma told me. Dad told me. I believe them. Even your obituary … .

Grandma had that tucked away in the missal—the prayer book—she used at Mass. Had it laminated.

I wonder what happened to that. I wonder what would have happened if … ?

Death sucks, God. People dying sucks. You have one sucky plan and sucky will.

Too many deaths. Too many gone too soon. Just too much … .

45

Two days later now. I didn't do any writing yesterday. Skipped a day. Claire said that was okay. She's my hospice nurse. I don't think I've mentioned her name.

Claire the nurse and Rosamie the social worker. Once a week. Different days. Each in her own way asking me if I would like to move into a hospice setting. An institutional one.

I say no, not yet. Not if I don't have to.

So I guess I don't. Not yet. So that's good.

Claire was here today and Rosamie will be here in two days. One for the body, one for the mind.

Oh, and one for the soul. I can't believe I've forgotten to tell you about Arthur. Really. My gears are slipping.

He's a fellow parishioner at Blessed Sacrament Church in the University District and brings me Communion twice a month.

Jesus-to-Go. We deliver.

I kid about this stuff but it means something to me. More lately. No surprise there.

Not that I'm afraid of God or of going to hell or such.

I like to think being dead is going to be really, really good. It's getting between here and there that gives me the willies.

It could get bad. Really bad.

I don't want to write about it and I don't want to think about it. You may have noticed I haven't mentioned what my medical problem is.

"Problem." Talk about your euphemisms.

Well, I don't think I'm going to tell you. I mean all the medical people know and all the health insurance people and all my three visitors …

No. Four. Meals on Wheels.

But I'm just not going to write it. These last few years it's been loss after loss after loss chipping away at me and who I am and I'm just digging in my heels here and …

I know it makes no sense. What I'm doing. I know. But I just can't.

I just can't.

I could ask the social worker about that. Social worker/counselor. But I'm pretty sure I know what she'd tell me "You don't have to."

Darned right.

She'd add: "And you can change your mind if you want to."

Good point.

I wish death would hurry up. I think I'm as ready as I'll ever be. Father Gus from Blessed Sacrament has been by a few times in the last six weeks. I don't think I've mentioned him. Older than I am. Eighties.

He anointed me. Anointing of the sick, one of the seven sacraments. Heard my confession, too, but there wasn't a lot to it. Don't have the old oomph or opportunity for sin. (Now that's just sad.)

I've had all of the sacraments now except matrimony and ordination. The first time I had the anointing of the sick was so long ago it was called the last rites. Vietnam. It was part of the package deal called "war."

All-inclusive.

Received it—the anointing—after I was wounded. Just enough to receive the sacrament and a free trip home. Often called "the golden ticket."

Maybe I'll do better tomorrow. With the writing. Pick a topic and stick with it for at least a little while.

Yeah, John, let's do that.

Okay, John, it's a deal and a date.

What topic?

Oh, cripes, I don't know. How about summer of 1967? The Summer of Love?

Uh huh. How about the summer of 1969? Boot camp.

46

I see that yesterday's writing wasn't clear. (Right. Only yesterday's.)

I mean the reference to the Summer of Love. San Francisco. No, I wasn't there. I was in Kenmore, Washington, working at Brookfield Washington Academy.

Sarge, Dad's buddy, got me a summer job there. I lived in a section of the basement with the other working stiffs. A room to myself. An eight-hour work day. Three meals daily. I had Saturday and Sunday off, but except for going to Mass with Murray I had nothing to do on weekends.

Sort of like now. Only now I can't get out without a lot of hassle and so I'm resigned to just stay in.

Retired and resigned and ready to be recycled.

"And unto to dust you shall return."

Anyway. I don't remember being bored on my days off or my evenings. Some guys watched television. Three networks and two local stations. Rabbit ears for reception.

I had some money for treats at the local store. Not a long walk. Dough from my shoe-shining business. Except for a can of pop and a candy bar, there was nothing I wanted.

Why didn't I go to the pop shack, where the vending

machines were? Must have been locked up and the machines empty. I guess.

I know what I did! Boy, am I slow at all this. And muddled.

I had access to the school library so I read a lot. It was a good escape for me. I'd try to keep it up after I enlisted—the reading, not the going to the BWA library …

Oh, my God! Eric! He and Pudge knew I was at school over the summers after our sophomore and junior years. I must have told them what I did. Not just what the job was but how I killed time. Or, really, wisely used time.

Extremely wisely for a sixteen- and seventeen-year-old.

Let me check something. Don't go away.

I did. I did mention here that years later Eric's contributions to BWA included a building named for me. It was the new library.

Nice, Eric. Only took me how many years to figure that one out?

And, of course!, some weekends I went to Eric's or Pudge's house. Their moms so kind to me. Their dads, too, in their own ways. A guy's way. That's how I would have described it back then. Concerned about my future. My career.

Not pushy. Just bringing it up now and then.

U.S. Army.

Vietnam.

I didn't waver.

Both had served in World War II. Mr. Matthews, a Marine captain in the Pacific. Mr. Hudson, an Army sergeant in an "all-Negro" troop washing laundry in Europe.

It wouldn't be until 1948 that Harry Truman said, "Knock that crap off." Probably in stronger language. An end to segregation in the military. In theory, although a true end to racism can't be legislated.

April 4, 1968.

I want to write about that tomorrow.

47

Friday morning, April 5, 1968.

Dr. Bradshaw opened the door to our classroom—trigonometry—nodded at Mr. Heller, and motioned for Pudge to come with him.

A room full of squirrelly sixteen- and seventeen-year-old Third Years but even we knew something was wrong.

I clenched my hands so tightly my fingernails were cutting into my palms as I started rocking forward and backward in my desk chair.

Given my history, I thought it was his mom, dad, sister or one of his brothers. It was something awful.

It was death. The death of a loved one. A dear one. An irreplaceable one.

And I was right.

I wouldn't see Pudge again until the afternoon of Wednesday, April 10. After the funeral. The funerals, plural.

He walked into our dorm room, shut the door, put his suitcase on his bunk, and just stood there. Staring off at nothing.

I was familiar with the view.

It was a death in his family. In a lot of families, especially

Black families.

The Reverend Martin Luther King Jr. was theirs. And they were his. In ways—I realized then and am sure of now— those who aren't African American can never understand.

I don't remember what I said to Pudge then, or what he said to me. If anything by either of us. Looking at his face was like looking into a mirror.

The complete devastation. The horrific pain somehow coupled with an overpowering numbness.

He sat on his bed.

"Mom and Dad said this is important," he whispered after a time, still not looking at anything. Anything external.

I waited.

"This getting back to school," he said. "My being here."

He shook his head a little and blew out a breath.

He looked at me

"Thank you," he said.

"What? For what?"

He tried to smile and his lower lips quivered.

I remembered the day we had met. Nineteen months ago. "Lips." What the guys at the front desk had called him.

"You're in the fight," he said. "A funny way to put a war founded on non-violence."

I nodded but I wasn't following what he was telling me.

"Well, G.I. Joe," he said, "it seems you and I are foot soldiers. My being a student here at BWA is what the Reverend King was talking about, preaching about, working so hard for until … ."

He was silent for a time.

"I don't know if I could have made it through the last year and a half without you," he said.

I still didn't say anything, not wanting to get in the way of his thinking and sorting and hurting.

"No," he said. "That's not right. I would have but it would have been so much worse. You and Eric. You."

This time his pause was longer.

"I'm sorry," I said. "I know there aren't words."

He looked up at me. So frightened. "Is it always like this?" he asked. "For you. Because of your dad and your grandma? Is it always going to be like this for me? He was family. We just loved him so much and were so afraid that something would happen to him. So frightened."

I nodded.

"And we don't know what we're going to do without him," Pudge said." We just don't know. My parents just don't know. I just don't know."

48

I can't remember back on that afternoon, I can't write the words I wrote yesterday, without tears. Without long, shaky breaths.

I knew that in less than a week Pudge had aged. Yes, some of it physically but most of it psychologically. Emotionally. Spiritually.

Along with Eric because of his medical problems, and me because of, well, no family, Pudge had joined the walking wounded. The three of us. Gimping along.

On the morning after the assassination Mr. Hudson had called the school and then driven out to get him.

Pudge and his family had watched the news on television and listened to it on the radio for the days he was home.

First a private memorial service in Memphis on that Friday. Then a second one in Atlanta.

A three-and-half mile procession.

And then a national public service.

Local services across the country, including a Mass at Pudge's parish in Seattle.

I didn't know about all those back then. Later, when I read

about Dr. King's death, his being killed and what followed, I thought about Dad's death. Grandma's. And even though I remembered nothing of it, about Mom's.

Dad had died in the spring of 1966. Grandma in the summer.

I was still in a state of blur in April 1968. And then Pudge was, too.

Some of the students—and faculty—were very considerate to both of us after Dr. King's death. Before that, both of us were just oddballs. One because of his race, the other because of his background. His social status. Or lack of it.

But even then, after April 1968, some students—and some faculty—were racist, classist jerks. Thoughtless, if not mean.

I don't want to go into details. Into instances. Into examples. Bigots aren't much known for their creativity.

It's all the same stuff. In little ways and big.

A thought. Maybe some of them were walking wounded, too. What did I know about any of them? Pretty much nothing. Maybe their dad drank too much and beat them up. Maybe their mom was hooked on prescription drugs. Maybe, maybe …

Well, maybe a lot of things you usually don't know about when you're a kid or a teen unless you're the kid or teen living with it. Trying to survive it.

As just a kid. Just a teen.

So much for anyone of any age to handle.

I suspect every member of the BWA student body of that period has had his teeth kicked in a time or two since then. By life. "Hello, teen. Young man. Middle-aged man. Old man."

Wham!

Wham, wham, wham!

So much pain. So much sorrow. So much of just so much. Another thought.

I bet I was a jerk to some of them back then. I was caught up in my own grief and upheaval that I didn't pay attention to anyone else's.

I didn't see it. And if I had, I doubt that I would have cared much about it.

Until Pudge.

And his mom and his dad and his sister and his brothers. That April, fifty-one years ago.

49

After the last couple of days of writing it's hard to bounce back with something upbeat.

I probably should, just for the sake of my own mental health.

Let's see. What haven't I talked about? Pre-BWA, BWA, U.S. Army/Vietnam, Granite Falls, U.S. Postal Service, retirement.

A life summed up in one incomplete sentence.

I'm more tired than I was seven weeks ago. I assume you've noticed I've been numbering each day's writing.

Okay. Top of the eighth. My life in review. My autobiography.

I wish I had been good at something. Excelled. A profession or skill or relationship or ... something. But I just don't see it. Not looking back. And I don't remember hoping for it, working toward it, when I was young.

No. One thing. Be a good soldier. Kill the enemy. Kill the ones, if not *the one*, who killed Dad.

That was still my goal, even as I was "a foot soldier and neophyte to the idea of non-violence." Pudge and his family had a tremendous influence on me but I had a prior commitment.

A prior conviction.

A pledge.

Oh, young John, if I could talk to you then with what I know now.

I suppose everyone at my age and this stage in life wants to do that. Talk to the kid, the teen, the young adult, they were.

Offer a different perspective. Some knowledge. A little wisdom.

But that takes time. Mistakes. Pain. Life.

I know I did kill some men. Wounded others. And I'm pretty sure there were some woman. And kids.

Intentionally for the "enemy." But the others ... .

"Collateral damage." Such a bland euphemism.

Doing that, doing something like that, affects a person. Most people. Just about all people but some are better at handling it. Or hiding it, for a time.

I could tamp it down. Cram it down. Cover it up. Drown it.

For a time.

But that takes a lot of energy. That takes a toll.

I kept a job, I hung on, I white-knuckled it, until I was in my early thirties. Then, exhausted, I gave up. Caved in. Surrendered.

And I was lucky. Really. Blessed. Truly.

I got the help I needed. Not "cured," but with the situation (now *there's* a euphemism) better managed. Not everything under control but with more control than before I got help.

Counseling, therapy, education, groups, meds.

A lot of work, a big commitment, an ongoing battle.

Mental healthcare professionals and fellow combat vets who didn't hesitate to call BS on me.

Talk about tough love.

Some of those vets didn't make it to twenty-five. Thirty.

Forty. Fifty. Sixty-eight.

Some, many, had it so much harder than I did in that jungle. Too damaged—physically, mentally, emotionally, spiritually—to survive.

Sometimes the difference was this mission instead of that one. This trail. This encounter. This mortar round. This … .

It can take years, decades, to finally be killed in war. Or, rather, by war.

50

The federal marshal stood tall before the unruly crowd. Tall and strong. A no-nonsense fellow. Star pinned to his chest, hat on his head, six-gun in a holster on a belt wrapped around his waist.

"Mr. Dillon," a slender man said as he limped up to his boss. His hero. "I think we got trouble." A high squeaky voice.

"I think you're right, Chester," the marshal said. Attempting a deep voice.

The two men slowly surveyed the people.

"It's a mob," Chester said.

"It is."

"An ugly mob," Chester said.

"It is."

"Especially that big fellow in the back," Chester said. "You see him?"

The people turned to look behind them.

"I do."

"The ugliest man in an ugly mob," Chester said and the people laughed. As did the man.

"Ugliest in the territory," the marshal said and the people

laughed more.

"Mr. Dillon … I'm a might concerned."

"Good reason to be," the marshal said.

"They could turn on us," Chester said. "Faster than … faster than … faster than ."

A beat, two beats, of silence.

"A schoolmarm telling Leonard and Jake to stop talking and pay attention," the marshal said.

More laughs.

"Yes, sir. Faster than that."

"Chester, we're sitting on a powder keg filled with dynamite, TNT, nitroglycerin and Department of Defense Dependents Schools mess-hall baked beans."

More laughs and a smattering of applause.

"Oh, Lordy, Mr. Dillon, what will we do?"

"Chester, the only thing we can do."

"Run?"

Laughs.

"Do what they hired us to do. Today we earn our pay, Chester."

"You go first, Mr. Dillion. You get paid more than I do."

Laughs.

"Chester we got to outsmart them. We got to outthink them."

At this point Chester slowing limping off to his right.

"Chester!"

"Sir." Quickly limping back.

"What these people want, what these people need, is a song."

"By golly, I think you're right."

"I'm always right, Chester."

"You're right that you're always right."

"Home," the marshal said.

"Home?"

"Ho-o-o-o-o-me," the marshal sang pseudo-basso-profundo.

"Ho-o-o-o-o-me," Chester sang, going for a squeaky soprano, bordering on a screech.

Then, together. "Home, home on the range, where the deer and the antelope play, where seldom is heard, a discouraging word, and the skies are not cloudy all day."

Followed by the first verse, the chorus, the second verse and then, an invitation from both marshal and deputy:

"Everybody sing!"

A final romp through the chorus, a rousing round of applause, cowboy hats offs, deep bows and ...

That's the way I remember it. The Halloween talent show at school. Third grade. Leonard and Jake. Marshal Dillon and Deputy Chester.

This probably isn't the actual script or ad-libbing.

But I'm sure we took first prize. Beat everybody, including the eighth-graders.

And when Mr. Wright, school principal and "ugliest man in the territory," handed us the ribbon he told us, and the faculty and student body, we were both expelled.

We all knew he was kidding.

Now, that's a happy memory.

That brings tears, too. Good tears.

51

It occurred to me after I wrote yesterday's material that Leonard was a Black kid. Or, at that time, a "Negro."

It's not that I pictured him white, it was just that Leonard was Leonard. I suppose in the way that Pudge was Pudge.

My best friend in grade school and my best friend in high school.

One of my two best friends in the Army.

I don't know what to make of it, if anything. They were all sharp and funny. Nice guys. Guys you—well, I—wanted to hang around with.

Leonard was gone before Christmas of that *Gunsmoke* skit year. His dad shipped out. His family shipped out. I have no idea where he is now.

I hope he had a good life. I pray he had a good life. Filled with family and happiness and success.

He came up with the idea for the skit and wrote it (as much as an eight-year-old can write one) and convinced me I could call Mr. Wright ugly.

The story of my life: people just disappear. One way or another. With or without me being there.

A lot of time, maybe most of the time, I feel like I could

just disappear and it wouldn't make even a ripple in the life of anybody else.

A loner. By nature and by circumstances. And sometimes that's not easy to be. Maybe especially when you're dying.

Okay, another topic.

I don't know how my going to Army schools worked. Grandma moved with us and she was the one who took care of me on base housing. Dad lived there, too. Then he would be sent someplace we couldn't be and we'd go to her house in Des Moines.

The eleven hundred block of Harding Road. Now Martin Luther King Jr. Parkway.

Martin.

Martin, Martin, Martin.

I don't know what happened with Grandma's house when she was away from it. Did someone stay there? A neighbor just keep an eye on it?

And a grandparent can be on base housing, too, to help with a minor?

I don't know if that was ordinary stuff or the exception. I do know this: It gave me the most stability possible for the first fifteen years of my life.

That foundation, that love, from both of them made a big difference. I'm sure of that.

Have I mentioned I get tired more easily these days? I think I did. I could go back and check what I wrote but ... What's the point?

Knock, knock.

Who's there?

You know who, John.

Back to Leonard.

Leonard Green. That's right.

I don't think I could come up with the first and last name

of anybody else I went to grade school with.

I should be able to do that, shouldn't? I mean, sometimes I spent a whole year in the same school, same class, in Des Moines. I suppose I used to remember some. Maybe not after Vietnam.

Scrambled-eggs brain.

Misty.

Not my memory. But Misty Brooks. Third grade. First crush.

I should have told Leonard we needed her in the skit. For the lady who ran the saloon in the television show.

Kitty.

Misty should have been Miss Kitty.

Such sweet, wonderful, little kids facing such promising lives.

Such a long time ago.

52

This morning I told Rosamie, my social worker, about Leonard and Misty. She's very kind. I mean Rosamie. But I think Misty is, too. I mean now, not just back then.

Hard to imagine that little girl and those two little boys in their late sixties.

Rosamie asked me if I thought the writing was helpful. I said sometimes with some stuff and she nodded.

She's got a fair share of wisdom for someone in her early thirties. I suspect she was born to be a social worker.

Some people, the lucky people, are born to be what they end up being. I mean the right career or vocation. A good person doing the good things they were created to do.

I suspect that always somehow involves helping other people. I look at my adult life and I don't see that. Not living what I was born to live. Whatever that was. Not much helping others.

Just day by day. Year by year. Decade by decade. Death.

I'm not complaining. (I hope I'm not. Maybe I am a little.) I have no doubt a whole lot of people have had—and have—a life much tougher than mine. Troubles and heartaches much bigger than mine.

I'm just saying ...

Suppose a pebble is thrown into a pond and it doesn't make *any* ripples?

It feels like that's me.

John "No Ripples" Eastman.

I kind of know that's not true. Wasn't I writing something about Pudge saying I helped him when he came back to school after Dr. King's death?

Okay. I did something when I was fifteen.

John "One Ripple" Eastman.

I'm not trying to focus only on the negative here. To wallow in crud. One of the (many) meds I take is supposed to help me from getting too low. I think it does.

In times past, I was a lot lower.

What I miss is going for walks—after I was discharged. Marching in boot camp and humping it in Nam was no fun. But when I got to Granite Falls, right after leaving the service, I could walk a long way. Hike a long way, through the woods. Cool, peaceful, forested foothills.

Then I got a postal route in North Seattle and I spent most of my workday on my feet. I'm not saying I liked it all day, every day but there's no way I could have survived an office job. An indoor job.

I'll tell you one thing the military prepares you for. Dealing with supervisors who are little dictators. Like a bad sergeant or psycho lieutenant, they can make your life miserable.

Of course, in the military that guy can see to it you're reassigned or eliminated. I mean ordered to take point one too many times.

The law of averages.

Life isn't fair and neither is death.

But, on the bright side, one of the skills I picked up in combat was a demeanor and look that said, "Do not ... fool ... with me." (That cleaned up for Grandma.)

I shot that stare at more than one dictatorial supervisor and then they left me alone. It wasn't like they could write me up or anything because I hadn't done anything.

Except of course, I had.

What could they say in their complaint? "Today John Eastman looked at me"?

.

53

I liked being left alone. No, I needed to be left alone. To do my job. Casing the mail and then heading out. Walking. Hot, cold, rain, sun, and occasionally snow.

Mile after mile.

House after house.

Year after year.

Never really getting over what happened over there.

Seldom, and then only temporarily, getting worse.

I was just a kid. Torn up by the death of his dad and his grandma. Then all the toxic horror that's war was thrown into the mix

Stop.

Stop, stop, stop!

Not today.

Yes, it was horrible but not today.

Christmas 1966. I wrote about Thanksgiving, right? Yeah. A little. I could say more about that. At Eric's house. And Christmas at Pudge's.

Compare and contrast. Okay.

At both places the food was so good. So very, very good.

But different. One from the other. I don't know how to put it. Upper-class white and middle-class Black? Separate traditional food and the same dish cooked in a different way.

Pumpkin pie and sweet potato pie.

Just thinking about them. About either one.

Everything, all I could eat. Both places. With leftovers, with raiding the refrigerator, at any time.

I didn't eat so much that I got sick but I really did have to loosen my belt. Discretely, I hope.

Did I tell you the Hudsons had a framed photograph of the Reverend King in their living room. On a bookshelf.

Huh. I just noticed that when I write about him I say "Doctor" King except when I'm doing that in relation to the Hudsons.

There he was always "Reverend."

That was important to them. A religious leader and all that entailed.

Yeah. A religious leader and all that entailed. That's what Pudge and his siblings learned.

Huh.

It occurs to me that I can't write "this is what rich white people do" and "this is what middle-class Black people do" based on just what the Hudsons and the Matthews' did.

Come to think of it, I can't write "this is what it's like to be a combat solider in Vietnam" or "deal with all the fallout of having been a combat soldier in Vietnam."

I mean not all those soldiers. Not all the guys who dealt with, deal with, having been over there and a part of that.

This is just me. Me with Eric's family. Me with Pudge's. Me in combat. Me after it.

I'm no sociologist, if that's even the right term or profession, who looks into stuff like this.

I never went to college. At all. And, to the best of my recollection, I never read a book about sociology or by a sociologist.

I'm not putting any of that, any of them, down. It's just

that I'm no expert beyond my own personal experience. And even that could be skewed by an iffy memory.

What the heck! Who inserts a disclaimer about himself written by himself and for himself?

Well, apparently I do.

Hey, John, why don't you want to write more about Thanksgiving and Christmas?

Oh, poop.

54

Apparently there's a lot I don't want to write about. Or that I want to just gloss over.

Is that okay? Am I supposed to muck around more in the parts that hurt? That hurt back then and, I'm pretty sure, would hurt now if mucked around with.

I already did some of that. Not just here but with counseling and therapy.

Here's something I learned. You may be very anti-counseling and anti-therapy until you reach a point where you are very anti-continuing to live.

Grace of God, *that* can be quite the motivator.

Grace of God, if help is available.

Grace of God, if booze and drugs haven't already fried your brain or destroyed some other part of your body.

I'd say I damaged a few of my parts but didn't destroy all them.

And, what?, I lightly sautéed but didn't fry my brain.

I do wonder if I had ancestors—or even some contemporary relatives I know nothing about—who leaned toward addiction. And I wonder if, minus those early deaths in my family and my going to war, I would have avoided it in myself.

Like the explosive material was there but the fuse was never lit.

I can see how my life could have been easier.

But who knows? Maybe I would have gotten hooked on pot and coke and worse if I had been a college student in the early 1970s. Maybe I would have found a way to get just as messed up/mixed up by something other than combat.

I have to say, when it comes to the latter, that really seems unlikely. I don't know what would be as efficient and thorough as carnage and death. Day after day.

So many traumas. So much stress. I don't see how anyone escapes that experience, those experiences, unscathed. Yes, to varying degrees but no one gets off, gets out, scot-free.

New thought. (No. Truly. A new one.)

There have been times in my adult life when the PTSD really hit the fan.

For instance, when I retired at age fifty-five and had time and disposable income. Nothing to do and a lot of time to think.

Hello, memories. Flashbacks. Anxiety. Dreams. Depression. "Self-medicating."

My retirement party, to put it politely, was really lame. A hastily-slapped-together-gathering. A hug or hearty handshake from a few fellow letter carriers but lots of quick waves and "See ya."

Not even that from the local stalag commandant. My immediate supervisor. She shed no tears seeing me go.

I strained not to make my goodbye a terse comment on what I really thought of her. She knew, unless she was incredibly stupid. So maybe she didn't know.

Nah. She wasn't stupid. It takes some brains to be that lying, vicious, back-stabbing, self-centered. Not to mention completely devoid of empathy.

Empathy! Poo. She couldn't even muster up a little

sympathy.

I didn't mention she played favorites. You probably just assumed so and you were right.

An idea:

"Dear God, give her peace and joy."

Really. "Give her peace and joy because she is one …"

No. I don't want to ruin it. My subversive prayer.

Double down!

"I forgive her, Lord."

Whoa.

55

That was some strange writing yesterday. I just reread it and I'm sticking by it. Bless her. I forgive her.

"Why the hell would you do that?" you may ask.

I did. Ask that. For the rest of yesterday and again this morning.

For a little while soon after I retired I saw some of my former coworkers from time to time. They'd tell me stories about her and it would cheer me right up.

Cheer me up a little but the other stuff (also mentioned yesterday) sort of destroyed any trace of cheer. The PTSD stuff.

There's a retirees club. Or used to be. A summer potluck. A Christmas gathering. I never made it to any of those. I suppose they still do that.

The effort—emotional and physical—was too much for me. It's been a long, slow slide getting to where I am today. I mean since the post office.

Whatcha been doin' since you retired, John?

Buncha meds. Prescription, I mean.

If you're only as old as you feel (I hate that saying!) then I'm old.

Age is just a number (ditto on the "hate that saying"). Yeah, as long as you've still got your health. Which, I'm pretty sure, I lost that at the age of fifteen. Goodbye, Dad. Goodbye, Grandma. Hello, orphanhood, grief, war, death, PTSD, terminal condition …

Did I leave anything out? Probably. But those are enough. Hell. I can't even wallow when I want to. That's pathetic.

Why can't you, John?

I think I'm talking to myself more lately.

And writing to yourself.

Bite me.

You were writing you can't wallow well.

Not being allowed to wallow is more than I can swallow.

Why "not allowed"?

Because through my cataract-dimmed eyes I can still see the truth of my situation, thanks to Grandma. And that is:

There are others much worse off than I am.

Their lives, past and present, *really* suck.

For example: My fellow vets now living on the street and more than hip-deep in mental illness, addiction, and poverty.

The unholy trinity. No, wait. With homelessness that's four things. For too many guys. (Yes, guys and gals.) Sign here, young fellah. Little lady. You're in the service now!

And for some of us, who served "only" two years give or take, we're never out. Never free from what happened, what we saw, what we did, during those twenty-four months. Or less.

I don't know how all this works but our brains are changed. Our memories are embedded. Our bodies are …

Wait. That's not me. The last one. My only physical "wounds" during that time were foot- and crotch-rot. And some half-assed wound—no, not in my ass—that got me sent home.

I walked off a plane back in the States. Was discharged. Got a job. Worked. Got another job. Worked. Retired.

Now I can look out my front window and see tents on the

sidewalk. Homeless. And how could they not be hopeless?

And here I am. Home, pension, impending death.

Two out of three ain't bad.

Huh, Grandma?

I started this writing stuff thinking it was about three years at BWA. It's been so long since I used those initials here I better say what they stand for: Brookfield Washington Academy.

I'm supposed to be figuring out, through jotting down a few reminiscences, whether or not I'll go to my fiftieth class reunion a little while from now.

I have decided I will.

And I have decided I won't.

I have decided I have to admit I'm undecided.

56

"Knock, knock."

"Who's there?"

Yes, we've already covered this. Death. But yesterday evening I started thinking about why I could write that I'm dying but not include anything about the cause.

The prognosis.

I don't know. I mean, I know what's killing me but I don't know why I haven't written it down here. Why I've kept it rather vague.

The doctors named it and explained it to me, as best they could to a non-medical person. My hospice nurse and hospice social worker have used the word, the words. And I've done the same with them.

So I considered this yesterday evening and decided to sleep on it. To toss and turn on it until a lovely med helped me slumber as best I can.

Then, this morning, I realized I still don't have an answer. No, that's not true. It's just that it seems like a silly answer. An illogical answer.

Which is:

I don't want to.

Coupled with "I don't have to" and "you can't make me."

I don't have a lot of control over my life. Few who are dying do. Few who have miserable chronic conditions. Few who are frail and fragile for whatever reason.

Good news! I'm really not concerned about my old age. (Here meaning eighty-plus.) Zero worries about that.

I wish I needed to be. But, as they say, such is … death.

So I'm just not going to put down the words for my specific medial situation. Not a single sentence on that death sentence.

Somehow, that makes me feel good. That smidgen of choice and freedom and power.

It's the little things that make life worth living. Even as the end rushes toward you.

And during this period of my life, the final countdown (10, 9, 8, 7 …), there are bits and pieces of my sixty-eight years that bring me comfort. Not just a laugh but, lately, a true sense of joy.

Well, at least *that* went right. Went really well. Went …

John "Jump Around" Eastman. Off on a new topic. (New tangent.)

Come along on John's Wild Ride.

Let's set the scene, shall we?

It was, oh, I guess the early 1980s. I was casing my mail (a final sorting and organizing before hitting the street) when the surname Nguyen popped up.

A very, very common Vietnamese last name pronounced like "win." At least that was what I had been told at some point over there.

It bothered me. The name.

"Hello, I am from Vietnam. My name is Win."

And my name is "Lose."

Lose. My mom. My dad. My grandma. My two best friends in Vietnam and all the fallout from my time there.

My life.

Nguyen.

This wasn't the first time I had someone with that name on my mail route. But it was somebody new on that particular block.

The Schmidts had moved out. The empty house had been for sale for a month or more. Now this.

There were other Nguyens on other blocks but … . I had gotten used to, if not comfortable with, that. With them. I could tolerate it.

Tolerate them.

"Them."

Barely.

That was the day I met Andrew.

Andrew Nguyen.

57

A-a-a-and we're back.

I thought I could just whip through the story, the memory, but it seemed some trouble breathing and some tears and a runny nose interrupted me.

None of them associated with my medical condition.

All of them tied to my mental condition.

I saw Andrew's eyes. His baby teeth. A smile.

I handed him a few envelopes addressed to that house, my action clearly against the USPS regulations, and hustled to the next one.

And the next and the next and the next.

I was out the following two days. Went to a doctor on the third and got the okay to miss more. A relapse. Not drinking or drugs.

Post-traumatic stress disorder. A term used since the late 1970s. A condition since … probably the first battle on the face of the earth.

Yes, many causes besides that. But that. Definitely that.

I'm trying to remember now how long I was out of work. Not enough to lose my job or even my route.

You know, or maybe you don't, too much time away can

get you reassigned to some piece-of-garbage route.

It occurred to me after yesterday's writing that I didn't actually meet Andrew until sometime later. That first day …

Hold the phone. I can see it in my mind.

I was moving right along, house to house, some stuff in my carrier bag and some in my hand, when the Nguyen mail made it to the front.

I glanced at the house and there was this kid in the front yard. Looking at me. But he didn't say anything. He scooted back toward the front door. Kind of an alcove. And he slipped behind some guy.

Some Vietnamese guy, a little younger than me, mostly in the shadow. Brown eyes. Unblinking.

Oh, man. That did it. All that therapy and I …

Never remembered that part.

Couldn't remember that part. I mean couldn't allow myself to remember that part.

Oh, God. I don't feel well. Right now. I really don't.

It's tomorrow. I mean from where I left off yesterday. Rosamie came this morning. Her regular appointment. And I told her about my little discovery.

I hate that. I mean everything, or a lot of things, whooshing back in like that. Out of nowhere but not out of nowhere. It's *inside*.

It's inside me.

I hate that.

Time doesn't heal all wounds. Sometimes it just cover some up. For a while.

Okay, I'm not going to write about that right now.

Here. This. Instead.

When I talked to Rosamie this morning about those brown eyes looking at me there were brown eyes looking at me. Southeast Asian brown eyes.

Rosamie is Filipino. Or, rather, Filipina.

And that, I mean her facial characteristics, has never

bothered me. I mean I never associated the way she looks with the way ...

When does life get easier, Lord?

When does it at least partially make sense?

When—not if—I get to heaven you have a lot of explaining to do.

Bucko.

58

I got an email from Eric this morning.

(Not to change yesterday's subject here. Yeah. Right.)

Still gently encouraging me to go to the reunion. He mentioned Pudge was going but I knew that.

I read the news, too.

What he, Eric, sent me a little while back was a list of all the guys in the BWA Class of 1969. I didn't recognize some of the names and couldn't recall all the faces.

Just as well. They were seventeen and eighteen when we parted ways. Now they're sixty-seven and sixty-eight. Bunch of old guys.

I had assumed most were retired, well-heeled, and enjoying the beginning of a long, luxurious final period of their lives. Peace and prosperity. So well earned ... or inherited. Or, I suppose, married into.

In any case, I have always thought they had it made. Even as pimply teenagers.

All of them but Pudge, Eric, and me.

Racism, frail health, and, well, you know.

And then Eric—that subversive, conniving, manipulative dear friend—sends me this second list. Not just names. Life summaries.

Items he had had "his people" research for me. (I believe I've mentioned he's a gazillionare. Give or take a billion.)

He, bless his heart, had assembled a short bio on each guy. Not quite a dossier but some life highlights. And the news that three have died.

Well … crap.

When what to my wondering eyes did appear, every single guy has been kicked in the teeth by life.

A few, like me, have had those teeth kicked down their throats.

I never would have guessed it. I never imagined.

Let me say here I think I've earned the right to a little me-me-me because of the hailstorm of … stuff … that has rained down on me.

Maybe I'll go to the reunion just to receive The Crappiest Life Award. (Which would come with a coffee-shop gift card. Expired.)

But, I have to admit, there are other contenders.

Death of same-sex partner by AIDS. (Gay at BWA during that time period. It must have been so awful, awful, awful for him. And for others at the school who were gay.)

Death of child from Sudden Infant Death Syndrome. (I'm sure a mom or dad never gets over that. Ever.)

Five wives, four divorces. (It makes me tired just thinking about it. How I hope the fifth one is happy and forever.)

Widowhood. (The end of a happy and "forever" marriage.)

Cancer.

Rehab.

Wife or son or daughter in and out of rehab.

Stroke.

Prison.

Bankruptcy and poverty.

Mental illness.

And on.

And on.

And on.

They run the gamut from "horrendous" to "worse than horrendous."

I don't think I would trade with any of them. My stuff for your stuff. My hell for your hell.

And that surprises me.

I guess I know mine and mine know me. So awful but not unfamiliar.

Even death at sixty-eight. Yes, it's the end of life on earth but it's also the end of all the pain. All the suffering. All the horrible negative …

But not the end of me. The me that is the most me, the truly me, is going to be with my mom.

Mommy.

Daddy.

Grandma.

I'm not afraid of dying. I've had time to work on getting ready.

A blessing.

I am afraid of the final scenes in the final act. I look forward to "there." As I may have already mentioned, it's getting from "here to there" that concerns me.

Meds helps. Chatting with God helps. Writing helps.

God dang Eric.

59

I think I'm ready to get back to Andy. To Andrew Nyugen, the little kid on my route. With whom I moved from being "Mister" to "Mister Eastman" to "John" to "Jake."

As he turned four then five and then moved away.

By then we were longtime buddies.

It happened this way:

After I got back from some time off and was working my route again he would come ripping out of the house and run up to greet me, take the mail, babble about something, and run back in.

I mean he spoke English. And Vietnamese, too. But, in my experience, all three-year-olds babble.

His mom would be watching from the front window. She got into the habit of waving and I started waving back.

Once in a while I thought I saw his dad standing farther back in the room. No wave there. Either direction.

One morning, after his fourth birthday, I was standing across the street, waiting for a car to go by when Andy popped out of the house, saw only me, and went racing toward me.

It still gives me the shakes. What could have been.

I yelled at him and motioned him to stop but four-year-olds aren't known for paying attention. To an "old-man" friend or a speeding car.

I met him half way into the street, scooped him up, and ran toward his house. The driver slammed on the brakes and skidded past where we had just been.

Andy looked scared and I looked scared and his mom tore out of the house, took him from my arms—he pretty much leapt from my arms—and crushed him in hers.

A lot of my. And then a lot of tears.

All the way around.

Including from Mr. Nyugen, who had flown out of the house and joined us.

The driver, a male teen, was out of the car and kept saying, "I didn't see him! I didn't see him!"

Mr. Nyugen stepped forward to me and very formally shook my hand. Terror on his face.

What might have been.

I'm sure mine looked the same.

What might have been.

Later I thought "what might have been" in Vietnam a decade or so earlier. For all I know we could have been on opposite sides, rifles aimed at each other, or at least aimed at where we thought the other might be.

The next day Mr. Nyugen and Andy were at the mail box. The dad formally invited me to a family gathering, a barbecue in their back yard, to be held two weeks later.

Andy did a bang-up job translating his father's words and added multiple times: "Hot dogs. Hmmmburgs. Izecreams."

I went. The menu was an incredibly delicious mix of Vietnamese and American food. It was obvious all adults among the extended family there had heard the story.

I suppose some of the kids, too. A cautionary tale.

I stayed just long enough not to be rude. After a bit, it did start to get to me but, overall and much to my amazement, for a brief time I was okay.

Then and there

I don't know why. Maybe because every time I saw the little guy, that sweet child, I was just so tremendously glad he wasn't hurt.

And everyone there felt that way.

When he was five the family moved away. Different city, different state, better job.

Obviously, I still think about him. Little Andy.

What a heck of a therapist he was. What a miracle worker.

60

I'm finding I like being surprised each day as I write these bits and pieces. (Am I using that expression too often?) No, that's not right. Sometimes the surprises hurt like hell.

Take me back to hell.

Deaths, orphanhood, boarding school, Army, war, combat, more deaths, winning-lotto-ticket wound, and back over here.

Man, I could write a book.

Ha!

Everyone could. By this stage, this age, in their life. I used to think the lucky ones were those died young. Mom. Dad. Dork. Buddha.

But now ... .

They missed out on a lot. Yes, a lot of pain but also a lot of figuring out what that pain is all about. Or at least thinking about it even if they didn't come to any big and brilliant conclusions.

I suppose most of us don't.

Little insights. Glimmers of grace.

I think that's the best we can do. The best I can do.

Being in hospice is like graduate school in theology and

philosophy. Or it can be.

Gee, John, generalizing much?

No, not like graduate school. More like an internship. A lot of work for what comes next.

Boot camp! It's like boot camp.

Sort of.

I've never gone through anything like it. Similes fall far short. Analogies droop. Metaphors … you get the idea.

For example: (Or "e.g." to be academic.)

A whole lot of thinking about the big picture. The huge topics and experiences. Life and death. What a pair.

"And now, for your entertainment and enjoyment in these finals days, we present 'Life & Death.' Let's give them a big round of applause."

I've prayed more. Read more Scripture. Read more books and websites on death and dying. Getting ready. Getting through this. Without being suicidal, just wanting to be done.

Wanting to be arriving. Stepping off the bus. Being greeted by those I knew and loved. And by those—family members—I never knew but I know I'll love, and who have been loving me. Have been waiting for me.

Happy thought: Dork and Buddha. "John? Jeeezus. What the hell happened to you, old man?"

I know, I know, that I don't know. This is just how I picture it. Imagine it.

But I'll tell you this: I think it's going to be better than I picture or imagine it.

I think there's something, I think there's everything good, beyond my time here. And that's true no matter what you believe about what's to come. Pearly gates or just a dirt nap. Into a new existence or the end of your existence.

We're all going to be pleasantly surprised.

Oh, my God … that sounds pretentious of me. The theological, philosophical, cosmological, saintly, John W. Eastman.

Who probably just used the word "cosmological"

incorrectly.

Cosmology? Cosmetology?

But, hey, I'm doing the writing and this is what comes to mind and what I've been thinking about so what're *you* gonna do about it.

Huh?

What?

Huh?

Yeah, that's what I thought.

(Insert crude and unkind word here impugning any challenger's character, strength, or courage.)

That's all big-picture stuff. Tomorrow we'll look at the little picture. Maybe

Who knows what the future may bring?

61

Have I mentioned sometimes I'm scared spitless about this dying stuff and take a lovely little pill to calm down?

I am.

I do.

And now, to continue.

Well, well, well. Still on track for an examination of the little things. Good for me.

Death and the Little Things, by John W. Eastman. Soon to be a major motion picture, starring whoever is a hot-stuff actor right now.

Not Walter Brennan.

Walter Brennan? Man, I'm old. But, it seems, not going to get very much older.

Did I already include him in here somewhere?

Yesterday and today I've been really loosey-goosey with this dying business. With this business of dying.

I'm just going to go with it. The writing. I've come to realize I shouldn't be worried about not being worried. Or feel bad about feeling good. I'll be okay about being okay.

It seems to me there's some Scripture quote (don't ask me specifics about the Bible, I'm a Catholic) about Jesus saying, "Hey, screw tomorrow's problems. Focus on how today sucks."

Sounds like a new translation.

But you know what I mean and, more importantly, I know what I mean.

Right here, right now, I'm okay.

All things considered.

I'll take that and—more— I'll thank God for it.

Thought:

I'm still able to think clearly. How frightening it must be for those realizing they can't. Those beginning to lose their cognitive functioning.

Terrifying for them and their loved ones. Terrifying— heartbreaking—for those loved ones even after that person has lost the ability to be aware of how much they've lost.

Help 'em out, Lord. It's not like it's gonna cost ya or kill ya.

Have I mentioned God and I have gotten pretty informal in speaking to one another? Not that I hear voices. Or a voice. Just that somehow I know ... I haven't got the words to describe it.

I suppose the best I could say is an awareness of a Supreme Being's presence and of his kind of getting a kick out of my at-first-glance irreverence.

Here's good news for you whether your dying soon or much later:

God has a sense of humor.

God invented humor.

For us. For you.

Oh, man, now I'm preachy.

Time to take up the collection.

Little things. I was going to write about little things. Okay. Sparrows. If that's what they are. Little brown birds.

62

A new day. Still feeling pretty much okay. But I know that can change in a heartbeat. In the blink of an eye. Change emotionally, physically, and a bunch of other ways. Spiritually. Okay, now to the birds.

The sparrows.

I can see them in some bushes right outside my dining area window. These days they bounce around, flit, in the new leaves. Spring-green leaves.

My last spring, I assume.

You know, or you probably don't know, it can take some work to reach this point when you're dying. Not like "we're all dying" but like tick-tock, tick-tock, tick ...

That's all folks.

For here and now. Yes, as I've said or I hope I've said, I believe in heaven and I believe I'll end up there but the unknown is always scary. And change is always hard.

Of course one's death is a giant ball of ... I don't know how to describe the feeling. The feelings.

Sometimes I wonder if Mom and Dad and Grandma had that. Over time for the ladies, wham for the gentleman. And for Dork and Buddha. Alive, wham, dead.

I hope I get to ask them. All of them. I think that will happen. What the hell good is heaven if it doesn't include stuff like that?

I don't know what kind of bushes they are. I mean outside my window. In the winter they have no leaves and some kind of seed pods. Or maybe it's the flowers growing in the bushes that have the pods. All winter-brown. Dry. Dormant or dead.

Holy smokes, I write the way a lonely, old man talks. On and on and on.

I didn't used to be this way. I don't mean old, but, yes, old. I mean a little Chatty Cathy. I think that was some kind of doll when my ... action figure ... of choice was G.I. Joe.

G.I. John. No empty head there. Not after ... No, it was packed with so much, let's call it "stuff," it took years, therapy, meds to ...

I think I've already written that. I apologize if I'm repeating myself. Another old-man trait.

With age comes wisdom. Kind of. With having been kicked in the heads many times, in many ways—that is, living a life—comes a sense of acceptance.

Yes, the bumps in the road but more so the bumps to your head.

Your heart.

Your soul.

My head.

My heart.

My soul.

My journey, my story, my life is unique, and at the same time, is like everybody else's. Details vary.

I'm pretty sure I wrote about Eric sending some information about the life of each member of the BWA Class of 1969. Or about a lot of them.

Bad stuff, sad stuff, horrid stuff. For some, decades of great joy. For others, moments.

I had years of good. Times of horrid.

At this point, and considering my health and prognosis, I'm tired. I look forward to resting.

Shoot! The sparrows.

I don't mean "shoot the sparrows," I mean "shoot, I still haven't finished my story about the sparrows."

63

I think most people are impatient. Not all. But it's the exceptional person who can calmly wait and wait and wait.

I'd like to think I've gotten better at it over the years but I really want to be done with this dying. Not take matters into my own hands but simply be through with it.

These days (weeks, months) I seem to have a lot of "Why am I still here?" thoughts.

Coupled with "Why *was* I here?"

My accomplishments seem meager. Or nonexistent. Maybe that's partly because of Pudge and Eric. Not that I begrudge what they did and what they do, more that they set the bar so high.

Without knowing they had done that.

I slept well last night so I woke up thinking more. Or thinking more clearly.

When I compare—"compare and contrast" as some school assignments used to instruct (demand)—those two are "way up there" and I'm ...

Not that I want, or wanted, fame and fortune but I would have liked to have done just ... more. To have been a person like Jim in Granite Falls, who took me under his (own broken) wing when I returned from Vietnam.

Like Pudge's mom or Eric's mom who made me feel at home when I had no home. Made me part of a family when I had no family.

I walked, wandered, wafted, through my life without touching—without helping—anyone. In too many ways, not even myself.

I don't think I blame myself. Well, not completely. I could have been a better guy but, to be honest here (I think I'm being honest here), I was dealt a really crappy hand.

To be just a kid without a family or home.

It's not an excuse but it's a ... what? Contributing factor. Yeah. That sounds about right.

Maybe *the* contributing factor.

Then add more than a pinch of combat, and stir.

Now it doesn't matter. So close to the end. So near to the beginning.

Your young men shall see visions and your old men shall dream dreams. Or some such. In the Bible. Somewhere.

Sophomore year. BWA. The dream. Turn eighteen and enlist.

Go to Vietnam.

Fight in Vietnam.

Kill in Vietnam.

Check. Check. Check. Check. Check.

My vision then.

Now, my dreams.

I could have gone to college. Not enlisted. And not been drafted because of a college deferment.

My high school grades were good. In those days, a college student could work part time and afford tuition, books, and a place to live. Then, too, there was Dad's life insurance money and my other nest egg ... eggs.

I bet I could have found a scholarship. I bet Eric's family would have found me one or funded one just for me.

Oh, how I wish I'd been kinder. To so many individuals at so many times in my life.

Silver and gold I have none but what I have I give to you: small or large, complex or simple ... an act of kindness.

Not that I wish my life had been better. More that I wish I had been better in my life.

With my life.

With those days, weeks, months, years, decades.

With those golden opportunities to be kind not overlooked, ignored, squandered.

64
Epilogue
by Eric Matthews

It's been three months since John William Eastman passed away in his bed on the night of June 13-14 and was found by his hospice social worker on the morning of June 14.

The day of our fiftieth class reunion.

As his primary contact person, I was notified in the early afternoon and immediately got in touch with Pudge who was already in town.

Used to being in the public spotlight, we knew the BWA show must go on but we were filled with grief.

I hadn't seen John since Christmastime. Based on his writing, I think he might have been a little confused about that. For Pudge, it was more than a decade.

We were both so looking forward to the three of us getting together on the evening of the 14th. Of walking the halls. Of swapping old stories and lies.

I was going to surprise them with a new portrait hanging in the refectory. The three of us as sixteen-year-olds. Looking like we did on an afternoon in late autumn 1967.

A framed target for students to lob food at if the power

suddenly went out in the middle of an evening meal. I suppose that doesn't happen anymore. The power is secure. The students are less unruly. Or, more likely, they have found other ways to be unruly. Their own ways, twenty-first-century ways.

After the formal part of the reunion gathering that evening, Pudge and I went to the refectory and stood in front of the most recent portrait, the latest among notable graduates since the school began.

We two already had individual portraits of us up there but we didn't pay any attention to those. We just stared at the newly-hung painting of three boys. Jake, Pudge, and me. Third year. Based on a photograph an underclassman had taken with my camera. For me. For us.

Jake, slender and tall, in the middle. His arms around our shoulders, his hands making bunny ears or devil horns behind each of our heads. The main school building behind us, its windows bathed in the golden reflection of that November sunset.

A glorious moment, some half century ago.

Remembering.

And our hearts ached.

I motioned to one of the men in my entourage and he reached into his suitcoat pocket and handed me two small, clear plastic bags. I knew there was a third in there that wouldn't be needed.

I gave one to Pudge who looked at it and smiled. We each pulled out some cold, sticky, cooked spaghetti noodles and flung them at the new painting. Several of them stuck.

Then we turned to each other, embraced, and laughed and cried.

* * *

I'm sure John, Jake, would want his life review to end with

that scene but that wasn't the end of his story.

I've had it published, using his pen name. It's the one he hid behind when he wrote hilarious, skewering columns in the school newspaper during our junior and senior years.

"Bill Dodds."

Bill, in a tip of the hat to his father, Sergeant William John Eastman. And Dodds, which I never understood until I read his life review. It's the acronym for Department of Defense Dependents Schools.

John had typed it at the top of the first page of his memoir. I've used it on this book's cover.

It bothered both Pudge and me that John felt he had had little or no impact on others. In fact, he touched, he helped, many, many people.

At John's funeral, held at Seattle's St. James Cathedral on June 17, Pudge spoke about this to the congregation and the members of the media there. My people (sorry, John, I know that sounds pretentious) let the public know a website had been set up for those who would like to share how John had bettered their lives.

And, because of my vast (and John would say "stinking rich and powerful") business network, I also initiated a search for those he wrote about or their loved ones.

Acts of kindness, golden moments, with which John, unknowingly, filled his life and the lives of countless others.

65
Epilogue II

"I don't know how an eight-year-old would know ... but Jake knew"

First, I want to thank Mr. Matthews for tracking me down and then sending me a copy of Jake's retelling of our *Gunsmoke* skit.

It's a happy memory for me, too, but I don't think he told it right. He came up with the idea and the needling of Mr. Wright, our principal. And he chose to be Chester.

I thought he should be Marshal Dillon but he said no. I would do a better job.

In a way, he sparked my career. Some years back I retired after a long time with the U.S. Marshals Service.

I missed him after Dad was reassigned and we had to move.

He was funny, coming up with things like calling Mr. Wright the ugliest when he was known for being a handsome fellow. I don't know how an eight-year-old would know it was okay to tease Mr. Wright like that but Jake knew.

I suppose it was instinct.

I was sorry to learn of his death. I would have loved to have visited with him. We didn't know each other for very long but he was a good friend.

Now, an older fellow myself, I would say he's a cherished memory.

—Leonard Green, aka Marshal Matt Dillon

"I admired his courage ...
and envied the dedication he had to his father"

I had been looking forward to seeing John at the class reunion although I fully understand why he wasn't keen on seeing me.

When I look back on my years at BWA I think "what a pompous ass."

Me, not John.

I wanted to tell him I'd changed. I'd grown up. I'd made costly decisions that were the right decisions. My father and I were estranged for the last thirty years of his life.

He couldn't accept having a gay son. And then a gay son with a life partner. And some years after my father's death, a gay son who married his life partner.

I want to be clear on this: I wasn't a pompous ass because I was, I am, gay. In high school I was a gay pompous ass.

I'm sure others will write about John's humor. It was brilliant. Aimed at me, a blistering—and in the long run, therapeutic—weapon.

But what I wanted to tell him at the reunion was how much I admired his courage and how much I envied the dedication he had to his father.

I had heard his goal—or maybe better put, his quest—came true and he went to Vietnam. I never considered what that really meant or how it must have affected him.

—Aston Aston III

"'Buddha' and 'Jam' … helped Donnie a lot"

My brother used to write us about "Buddha" and "Jam" and those two helped Donnie a lot. It was clear they were helping him and watching out for him.

I couldn't stop crying when Mr. Matthews sent us John's memoir and what he wrote about Donnie.

Sometimes in the past, I couldn't stop myself from coming up with images of how he must have died. A slow, horribly painful death all alone.

Now I know that isn't true and knowing is better than not knowing.

It brings me great comfort to think of those three "kids" together again.

Someday I'll be there, too, and Donnie can introduce me to his buddies.

—Ellen Baxter Johnson

"He treated me like a young, intelligent, competent woman"

I have so many wonderful memories of John. When I met him, I was a timid schoolgirl. When we broke up, I was a young woman stepping out into the world.

I can't list "he did this and he did this and he did this" but I know he did.

It must have something to do with discovering my own self-worth because he thought so highly of me.

He treated me like a young, intelligent, competent woman, and as one, I came to realize neither of us was ready to be married.

And we shouldn't marry each other.

I think we both knew that.

But how I cried when we broke up!
—Marilyn Orlowski Petrich

*"When our mailman saved me,
he saved my father, too"*

I suppose the reason I remember John grabbing me up and taking me to my mom is because the grown-ups were so frightened by what almost happened. My dad was afraid and the only other time I remember him looking that way was when Mom died three years ago.

I read how I helped John but he didn't know how he helped Dad. Emigrating from Vietnam was so complicated. It was so emotional. It was so many things I never experienced.

I think Dad hated all Americans and trusted none of them, except John. Until John. That was a beginning. I suppose it could be said when our mailman saved me, he saved my father, too.

—Andy Nyugen

"I tell them a little bit about John"

I usually learn something from most of the hospice patients I work with, but John was special.

His life review is a treasure that, I suspect, will help many, many people. Both those who are nearing death and their loved ones.

I have often been asked about my profession. Don't I find it very grim and depressing?

Now when that happens, I tell them a little bit about John.

—Rosamie De Guzman

"Eternally grateful"

I would not be who I am, I would not be where I am, without John "Jake" William Eastman.

Dearest Jake, I'm eternally grateful to you.

—Edward Hudson, Pope Martin VIII, Pudge

ABOUT THE AUTHOR

Bill Dodds, the author of some three dozen books, attended an all-boys boarding school from freshman through senior year. (From "first high" through "fourth high.")
He graduated in 1970 but—pandemic!—was forced to place *Golden*'s main character in the Class of 1969. No in-person fiftieth reunions in the summer of 2020.

In 1974, Bill married the younger sister of two older schoolmates. Monica makes a cameo appearance in *Golden* in Chapter 30 as the director of Meals on Wheels.

She passed away from uterine cancer in 2013.

Bill writes:
"I would not be who I am, I would not be where I am, without Monica Faudree Dodds.
Dearest Monica, I'm eternally grateful to you."

BillDodds.com
wfdodds@gmail.com

20210109

www.ingramcontent.com/pod-product-compliance
Lightning Source LLC
Chambersburg PA
CBHW050937120626
46552CB00001B/244